WINSLOW'S
JOURNEY

WINSLOW'S JOURNEY

ELLSWORTH JAMES

WINSLOW'S JOURNEY

iUniverse books may be ordered through booksellers or by contacting:

iUniverse
1663 Liberty Drive
Bloomington, IN 47403
www.iuniverse.com
844-349-9409

Because of the dynamic nature of the Internet, any web addresses or links contained in this book may have changed since publication and may no longer be valid. The views expressed in this work are solely those of the author and do not necessarily reflect the views of the publisher, and the publisher hereby disclaims any responsibility for them.

Any people depicted in stock imagery provided by Getty Images are models, and such images are being used for illustrative purposes only. Certain stock imagery © Getty Images.

ISBN: 978-1-6632-0918-4 (sc)
ISBN: 978-1-6632-0920-7 (hc)
ISBN: 978-1-6632-0919-1 (e)

Library of Congress Control Number: 2020920975

Print information available on the last page.

iUniverse rev. date: 11/03/2020

To Kathleen
Love Of My Life
Sine Qua Non
F.A.T.E.

Not all those who wander are lost.
J.R.R. Tolkien, The Fellowship Of The Ring

Going to the mountains is going home.
John Muir

PROLOGUE

He was flying.

His body rocketed through the sky, miles above the earth. His arms swept back like the wings of a fighter jet. Face contorted into a rictus of exhilaration as he sliced through the night air. His eyes compressed into slits as he peered into the blackness. The onrushing airstream buffeted his ears like a thousand thundering hooves. A colorful necktie slapped against his chest. A shoe detached from his foot and was gone. He emitted a hoarse yell of joy, washed away by the onrushing wind.

Tilting shoulders and cupping a hand, he arced his body into a graceful banking turn. The movement was effortless, like an eagle floating on a warm thermal high above the earth. Enjoying the sensation, he shifted slightly and sailed in the other direction. He raised his head, enraptured at the sight. A billion stars filled the night sky, and a billion more were stacked behind them. Glittering celestial bodies extended into infinity, appearing so close and dazzling they stung his eyes.

He looked towards the earth and saw a shimmering blackness that appeared fluid, like a dark ocean. Rising and falling. Pulling at him. A warning bell sounded somewhere in his head, cautioning him to avoid the darkness. He swiveled his hands like aircraft flaps and urged his body upward, towards the heavens. Something began pulling at him, like a giant magnet drawing him to the earth.

His body began a downward glide. He strained against it.

Shrouded shapes rose from the darkness.

Then a glimmer of recognition, a dawning of awareness as the whirring mechanisms of his mind clicked into place. In the span of a heartbeat, it made sense. The shock of reality electrified his body, and a convulsion of terror seized him. He uttered a guttural scream that was ripped away by the wind.

He wasn't flying.

He was falling.

His body lost its aerodynamic contour and began to cartwheel as he plunged towards the earth. A shadowy mass rose to meet him. Dark tentacles extended upwards. Waiting to embrace him. He continued screaming as he struck something hard and unyielding.

He felt the sensation of things grabbing and slapping at him. Then the shock of collision, an eruption of fiery pain. His mind exploded in a starburst of yellow and red.

His world went dark.

CHAPTER ONE

Air Traffic Control Tower
Seattle Tacoma International Airport

Bob Childress never saw the catastrophe barreling towards him.

The man's broad face contorted into a frown of concentration as he stared into the radar screen and studied the crowded sky. Childress had thirty-two aircraft in holding patterns above the airport, with eighteen more queued up and awaiting departure clearance. The evening was a warm one in northwest Washington, with crystal-clear skies and a balmy breeze gusting in from the Pacific. It was a perfect evening for flying, and a busy one for an air traffic controller at Sea-Tac airport.

Childress directed his attention to the bird currently slotted number one in the landing queue, an Alaska Airlines Airbus completing a six-hour run from Honolulu. He checked ground radar to ensure the runway and taxiway were clear, then called the pilot and cleared the flight for landing. Childress watched as the aircraft turned into its final approach while keeping a close eye on the Delta 787 Dreamliner lumbering down the center runway and taking too long to get airborne. Childress punched their projected paths onto his monitor, and the icons of the two planes begin flashing red.

"Alaska three niner two…move away…repeat, move away."

The pilot did not return communication, although Childress' scope displayed the aircraft's arc as it pulled up and began a sharp climb. He waited until the sluggish Delta flight was airborne before again contacting the Alaska cockpit. "Alaska three niner two…climb to 5000 feet… proceed to cascade intersection…hold northwest as published…ten-mile legs…expect clearance at 2215."

He'd advised the pilot in controller jargon to route his aircraft in an elliptical pattern above the field until the runway cleared. He received grumpy affirmation from the cockpit, then Childress watched as the plane rose and banked to the west before turning his attention to other matters. In addition to the stack of aircraft overhead, he had a long line of passenger jets burning fuel as they idled on the airport's three primary runways. Childress also kept a watchful eye on the bevy of private and commercial aircraft queued up on an auxiliary runway and waiting their turn to get underway.

Childress spent his shifts in a large windowless room on the ground floor of the Terminal Radar Approach Control Center, called TRACON. The two-story building occupied a stretch of flat ground between the Cascade and Olympic mountain ranges. Seattle lay fourteen miles to the north, and Tacoma eighteen miles in the other direction. Towering Mount Rainier rose squarely within TRACON's airspace, and nearby Boeing Field dumped a steady stream of aircraft into the sky.

Bob Childress' job was the most demanding in commercial aviation and one that perfectly suited him. An honor graduate of the FAA Academy, he was a man fascinated with aircraft. He'd built model planes as a kid, studied aeronautics in high school, and completed ground school as a teenager. Himself a licensed pilot, Childress read tech manuals for pleasure and flew his Cessna on weekends.

Childress turned his attention to the commuter airplane idling on the auxiliary taxiway along the far side of runway three. Air Pacific Flight 272. He scanned the little bird's flight progress strip, a computer-generated record that detailed its flight plan. This one was a regional flight operated by Seattle-based carrier Air Pacific. The craft had been sitting twenty minutes, waiting to squeeze into the string of behemoths crowding the runways. Childress ran his eyes across his screen and saw a tiny break in the departure queue. It was time to send Air Pacific on its way.

"Air Pacific two-seven-two, you are cleared for takeoff runway 34 Right."

Childress received affirmation from the cockpit, then he flipped on the video feed and watched through the monitor as the EMB 120 twin-turboprop taxied onto the runway and accelerated into liftoff. A minute later, the aircraft was airborne and initiating its climb to cruising altitude.

Childress turned his attention to the next bird in line.

Over the next twenty minutes, he occasionally glanced at the green blip of Air Pacific flight 272 as it worked towards the end of his sector. The aircraft reached a vector altitude of 28,000 feet and would maintain this elevation for three hours before beginning its descent into San Francisco.

Fifty miles west of Sea-Tac, the aircraft would drop off Childress' screen. Controllers at Salt Lake's Air Control Center would take over and track the flight until ground controllers in San Francisco guided it to the ground. When the Air Pacific flight reached the boundary of Childress' sector, he advised the pilot to call Salt Lake traffic control.

"Have a nice flight," he said into his mike.

Childress returned to his busy screen and broke off without awaiting a response from the cockpit.

CHAPTER TWO

He awoke in a world he did not recognize.

Curled into a fetal position, body embedded in a shallow crater formed by the force of striking the earth, he strained to force open his eyes. He ran a hand across his head, which pulsed with pain. Swollen and misshapen, his skull felt as if it had been cleaved with an axe. His exploring fingers found the knot on his forehead, a sunken area below the cheekbone, and a ragged gash across his nose. Something crusty covered much of his face, and his hand came away dark with dried blood.

He moved his body fractionally, and a current of pain ran up his spine. His back arched into a spasm of agony and he lay motionless until it released. He extended a hand and explored his body. The right side had absorbed most of the punishment. The leg swollen to the size of a tree trunk. The knee issued a warning flare when he tried to bend it. An ugly ridge ran across his ribs, which radiated pain with every breath.

He heard a low babbling sound, a distant murmuring

as if people were in conversation. He turned his head in the direction of the noise and spotted the creek. His throat was sandpaper dry, and all he wanted was to drink from the stream. He extricated himself from the crater and turned onto his belly, then rose onto an elbow and used his arm and shoulder as a fulcrum to drag his body towards the water. After an eternity of crawling, he arrived at the creek and plunged his face into it.

The crater from which he'd emerged lay beneath a stand of enormous trees ringing a meadow filled with wildflowers, and the little creek ran along its perimeter. He wrinkled his nose as he caught the acrid smell and saw a blue plume rising above a low ridge at the far end of the meadow. He began moving towards the smoke, inching crab-like across the field. After an eternity of crawling, he arrived at the ridge and peered over.

"Oh, God," he said.

Wreckage was strewn across the field.

He spotted the twisted fuselage embedded in a tall conifer, wing and engine still attached. The plume of smoke rose from its smoldering turbine. Scattered around were blue seats and shredded clothing. Papers fluttered in the wind. Mangled engine parts littered the field. Wires and cables, and things he couldn't identify.

There were bodies.

A dozen broken forms lay scattered across the field, twisted into impossible shapes. Limbs torn away.

A severed head and eviscerated torsos. He called out to them, his croaking voice echoing across the field of bodies. There was no sign of life -- no movement, moans or screams for help.

A stream of disconnected images bobbed into his mind. He couldn't organize it into anything that made sense. The horrific scene and effort of trying to think caused a wave of exhaustion to ripple through his body. He closed his eyes and dropped into sleep. He awoke hours later, feeling no less confused.

He removed a wallet from his filthy and blood-crusted pants. He raised the driver's license to his eyes and stared at the photo. He didn't recognize his name or address. The wallet held a few credit cards and some cash, but nothing personal.

He put away the wallet and began a reconnaissance of the crash site, crab-crawling back to the fuselage. He spied an open hatch and gingerly pulled himself into the aircraft's cabin. In the cockpit lay a pair of mangled bodies. He crawled further into the plane and spotted an overturned beverage cart, the floor around it littered with food – bags of peanuts and crackers, candy bars and fruit, soft drink cans, and bottles of water. He tore open the bags and greedily ate his fill before slumping to the floor and falling asleep amidst the rubble.

It was dusk when he awoke and crawled to the open hatch. Lacking the strength to lower his body from the fuselage, he leg-rolled and dropped to the ground. A lance of pain spasmed through his body, and he lay moaning until it passed. Rising carefully to hands and knees, he crawled to the edge of the meadow and settled against a tree. As he closed his eyes and drifted towards sleep, he sensed movement in the periphery of his vision and heard the crackling of breaking branches.

Across the meadow, something large and dark pushed through the underbrush. A rhythmic huffing floated through the air like a steam locomotive.

He saw the hump between the animal's shoulder blades, the broad flat head and dished face, and the tan fur tinged with silver. The bear moved ponderously through the field, body swaying languidly as it swiveled its head from side to side. An uneven patch of white covered its flank, as if the animal had brushed against fresh paint.

The bear bent to the ground to sniff, rooted at the dirt with massive claws, then raised its snout and inhaled the breeze. It lifted its ears and swiveled its head in his direction, looking into his eyes. Helpless to defend himself and more curious than afraid, he returned its gaze and awaited his fate.

The bear studied him, its wide nostrils flared as it processed his smell.

It turned and rumbled back into the forest.

CHAPTER THREE

Sarah Winslow swayed in rhythm to the bass notes blasting through her headphones as she sorted through garden tools. Selecting a trowel, she used it to loosen the sun-baked earth, scooping out a handful of soil and using a ruler to precisely measure the hole's depth before setting in the plant. When the bud union was exactly an inch above ground level, she dragged over the garden hose and infused the ground with water.

Sarah wasn't a tall woman, barely an inch above five feet in stockings. A natural brunette, her pixie bob was currently blonde with pink highlights. Her face was oval, and her eyes a blue-green hazel. She kept in hot pursuit of youth through facials, health club workouts and Pilates. Today she wore her usual gardening attire: canvas sneakers, jeans, and tee-shirt covered by a colorful smock. A floppy hat and sunglasses shielded her face, and gloves protected her manicured hands.

She'd worked all afternoon at a task that should have taken thirty minutes. Repeatedly digging up and replanting the same bush, she wasted more time by throwing down the spade and dancing to any irresistible beat that rocked through the headphones.

She rubbed her neck and glanced at the afternoon sun, deciding she was done planting roses for the day. Sarah pulled off her wireless headphones and disconnected the Bluetooth. The music boomed from her phone. Shedding clothing as she danced, she adjusted the temperature in the outdoor garden shower and sang along with Donna Summer as warm water splashed down her backside.

She padded naked into the house and stood in front of the Sub-Zero, studying a stack of black plastic containers before deciding on Antipasti salad. Sarah slid onto a barstool and stabbed at the salad while flipping through a purchase contract for the seven-figure sale of a big house in Paradise Valley. It would bring a nice commission. She rubbed and twisted her neck as she scanned the paperwork. Wine was her go-to muscle relaxant, and she poured a generous splash from an open bottle.

She swirled the wine and watched the agitated liquid run down the inside of the glass. She impulsively drained and refilled her glass before moving to the bedroom. Climbing into bed, she sipped wine as she reviewed her day. She swore as she jumped up and ran to the bathroom. Popping the cap from an amber container, she shook out two pills and washed them down with a last swallow of wine.

She returned to bed and saw the note propped against his pillow. In no mood to deal with it, she turned off the light.

The chime of the phone awoke her.

She raised it to her ear and heard the voice of a stranger. She closed the phone and sat in darkness, wondering if she might be dreaming. She checked her call log, saw the inbound and outbound calls, then she punched in her husband's number. It rolled to voicemail, and she hurriedly dialed again. After the fourth attempt, she threw on clothing, grabbed her purse, and ran for the car.

Sarah arrived at Sky Harbor Airport as an orange-tinged dawn rose above the city. Tires squealed as she drove up the spiral ramp to the parking garage. The morning was already hot and sweat rose on her forehead as she jogged into the terminal building. A sign directed her to the airport's administrative offices, where a serious young man pointed to a row of molded plastic chairs.

A door swung open, and a woman walked towards her. Middle-aged, short, big glasses and retro-style Barbie hair. Wearing pajama bottoms and a hoodie sweatshirt, she had the rumpled look of someone roused from sleep. Dabbing at eyes with a wadded tissue, she offered Sarah a crooked smile and nodded as if they knew one another. Sarah heard her name called and the young man ushered her into a conference room.

Two men stood behind a desk. Solemn and wearing grim expressions. One opened a folder and shuffled through papers, then raised his head and cleared his throat. She interrupted him with a raised palm.

"Before you start," she said, "are you certain this involves my husband?"

"Let's make sure, ma'am," he said, shuffling more papers. "Has your husband traveled recently to Seattle?"

Sarah looked out a window and watched a jumbo jet roll past in slow motion. The whole scene felt unreal, unrolling in slow motion. She fought off the urge to scream hysterically. "He's in Seattle for a conference," she answered, hearing the tremolo in her voice. "He's not coming home until the weekend."

"Yes, ma'am. But according to our records, yesterday your husband bought a ticket for our Air Pacific Flight 272. He conducted the transaction online. We have an electronic receipt. Last night at approximately 9:30 p.m., your husband, Evan Winslow, boarded a flight bound for San Francisco and then Phoenix.

"That aircraft departed Seattle-Tacoma Airport at just after ten p.m. Pacific Standard Time. The manifest listed seventeen people aboard, including the pilot, co-pilot, flight attendant, and fourteen passengers including your husband." Sarah leaned forward and read from the Air Pacific badge that the man's name was Warden. He was short and wiry, with a trim mustache and shaved head. Warden punched a button on a remote and a map of the west coast appeared on the wall behind him.

An arcing red line ran from Seattle to San Francisco. Somewhere south of Portland, the path changed from solid red to dashed. A circle marked where the solid line ended and the dashed line began.

"This was the aircraft's projected flight path, which called for a two hour and fifty-minute flight to San Francisco. Scheduled to arrive at 12:50 a.m. After a thirty-minute layover, it would continue to Phoenix. Ground controllers at Sea-Tac tracked the flight until it reached their grid boundary and disappeared from screens. This occurs with every departing flight, and the controller saw nothing unusual about this one."

Sarah studied the map, trying to comprehend what possible meaning it could have for her. "Okay," she said. "What does this all mean?"

"Salt Lake controllers didn't pick up the aircraft," Warden said. "The issue wasn't noticed until 12:30 a.m. when it failed to enter San Francisco International airspace."

"Where did it go?"

"We don't know."

Her brows knitted in puzzlement. "You lost an airplane full of people?"

"We haven't lost it," Warden said. "We just haven't located it."

Warden must have realized the stupidity of his remark, as he flushed and nodded towards the other man in the room. "I believe Mr. Kelly can better explain."

John Kelly was a rumpled bear of a man, tall and overweight with broad shoulders and a sizeable gut straining over his belt. His thinning hair was tousled, his face sincere and holding a kind smile.

"Aircraft sometimes disappear from radar screens, ma'am," he said, "usually due to technical glitches, and we always find them. We know this one didn't land at any public airport between Seattle and San Francisco, because we've checked every registered field in the northwestern United States."

"Are you saying it crashed?"

Kelly shook his head. "Not necessarily. This plane has sufficient fuel capacity for nine hours of flight and might still be in the air. It's most likely on the ground. I'm betting it's parked at a little out-of-the-way airstrip."

"Why haven't they contacted you?"

"Good question," he said. "We know the flight crew didn't activate the plane's emergency locator system, which is a good thing. I'm sure this is a routine equipment malfunction."

"Then why call me in the middle of the night and scare me half to death?"

"Because," Kelly said, "we can't rule out the possibility of a mishap."

"By mishap, you mean a crash?"

Kelly said nothing.

Sarah felt a crushing weight descend on her chest as if gravity had intensified and was applying immense force, pulling her to the earth and sucking all available breath from her lungs. Tears began streaming down her face. Kelly pushed a box of tissue across the table and murmured consoling words.

"We have a chaplain down the hall," he said. "Would you like me to call him?"

Sarah shook her head and felt an urgent need to go home. She hurried from the office and sped across town, weaving recklessly through traffic and ignoring lights, repeatedly commanding Siri to call her husband's number. Screaming his name as she charged into the house. Running through rooms looking for him. She returned to the kitchen to pour a glass of wine and took it with her into the bedroom.

She fortified herself with a large swallow of the wine, then she unfolded the note and read it.

"Oh, my God," she said.

CHAPTER FOUR

He awoke to a nightmare.

Paralyzed. Flat on his back, arms folded across a heaving chest, body cadaver-stiff and frozen in place. A surge of panic caused his heart to rev up and set his pulse to hammering in his ears. He became aware of sensations around him. A distant hum and the light breeze ruffling his hair. The creek murmuring like whispering voices. Birdsongs in the branches seeming to carry a faint classical melody. He blinked open his eyes, then slammed them shut as harsh triple suns burned into his face.

Something was holding him down. He strained like a wild man against it and eventually wiggled a finger. This tiny movement released his body from its restraints. The triple suns coalesced into one, forest sounds returned, and he was able to prop himself upright. He gingerly stretched out and this time his back didn't spasm. The throbbing knee felt tolerable. He crawled to a nearby tree and pulled himself to his feet, staggering like a drunk but able to walk.

He rested awhile before hobbling to the debris field, where he gathered clothing, shoes, and a Seattle Mariners baseball cap. He ferreted out a cigarette lighter, flashlight, and small folding knife.

He felt better after changing into clean garb and pulling on hiking boots. A size too large, but serviceable. He collected magazines and newspapers from the wreckage and picked up an armload of dead branches, piling it into a teepee. At dusk, he lit the pile and watched the flames rise into the night.

He slept in snatches, spending the wakeful hours staring into the dark sky. He resumed rummaging at morning's first light. Locating the cargo hatch, he ran his hands around the edge until finding the recessed handle. A small tug and the hatch popped open. He hoisted himself inside and began tossing out suitcases and duffle bags, backpacks stuffed with gear, and elongated hard cases.

He examined his jackpot. Every suitcase contained field and survival gear. Duffel bags held camouflage clothing and heavy boots. He found camping equipment, tents and sleeping bags. Lighters and matches. Flashlights. Hunting knives. Fishing rods and tackle. Dehydrated food. Camping pots and pans. Wallets and fanny packs. A couple of pistols and dull green metal boxes filled with ammo. Cell phones. He rummaged through a shaving kit and found a small mirror. It seemed that every passenger packed cigars and booze.

The long cases provided the bonanza. He removed a rifle from one, and the odor of gun oil filled his nostrils. The scent triggered a string of images. Sitting on the plane, noisy men filling aisles around him, unshaven and smelling of the woods as they drank and bragged about their conquests. One bagged a moose, and another brought down an elk with a single shot. Enormous fish grew larger with each telling. Filled with bonhomie, they invited him into their liquor-fueled circle of brotherhood.

All now dead, their mangled bodies scattered across a field of wreckage. In death, giving him a chance at life. He removed the rifles and peered down the barrel of each one. They felt heavy and lethal in his hands. The model and caliber etched into the barrels. He chose one and rummaged through the green box for cartridges. Encased in copper-coated jackets with Teflon tips, the shells had the appearance of tiny missiles. He loaded the rifle and leaned it against a tree, less worried now about the grizzly.

He loaded and strapped a pistol around his waist, then he set up camp. He erected a tent and unrolled a sleeping bag. As the sun dropped behind the horizon, he ignited a pile of wood and watched yellow flames dance into the night. He banked the fire with larger pieces before burrowing into the bag.

He awoke to bright morning sun and a putrid smell. He tied a tee-shirt over nose and mouth. Kneeling beside a corpse, he searched the man's pockets. Rolling the body onto a blanket, he dragged it behind the fuselage and went back for another. He spent the morning engaged in the task of collecting bodies. He removed the pair strapped into the cockpit. Arranging the corpses in a row, he covered faces with blankets and jackets.

He tried to understand why he was alive and these men dead.

He followed the line of drag marks to a massive pine tree. Beneath it an indentation in the earth. Sunlight streamed through an oddly shaped space in the tree's crown. He gazed at the opening, and memories flashed into his head. The sensation of falling. Wind on his face. Something slapping and grabbing him. Then flashes of color. He had no memory of striking the earth.

He returned to camp and went through wallets and fanny packs. He looked at every man's identification card. Studied their faces. Each had someone praying for their return. He stowed the cards in the backpack before removing his license. His name was Evan

Winslow. He was forty-two years old and lived in Scottsdale, Arizona. Beyond this scant information, he knew nothing about himself.

He hobbled to the fuselage and searched through the chaos until locating a boarding pass. Dated June 12th. Listing Seattle as the departure city. Destination San Francisco. He found a leather portfolio behind the pilot's seat. It contained navigational charts and a spiral-bound notebook containing route maps.

He ran a finger down the Seattle to San Francisco route. It ran along an area of forest lying parallel to a long mountain range. He looked through the cockpit window and spotted a string of snow-capped peaks, comparing them to elevation depicted on the map. He chewed a lip and estimated distances.

Two hundred miles from civilization.

After an afternoon of staring into an empty sky, he began collecting gear. A nylon backpack on a lightweight aluminum frame. A pair of canteens, matches and lighters, a little tin coffee pot. Metal bowl and tin cup. A large hunting knife. A folded blue tarp, a lightweight tent and sleeping bag. He threw a travel tote fishing rod and a plastic tackle box on the stack. A foldable shovel and hatchet. He added a supply of liquor and cigars to the pile. Salvaged cell phones. Another box of cartridges.

He quit at dusk and lit the fire. Pouring a shot of bourbon into a tin cup, he ignited a cigar and considered his situation. Days had passed. The sky was empty. The forest silent. Nobody had come for him.

Two hundred miles.

He drained the cup and poured another shot, wondering if he was about to do something foolish.

CHAPTER FIVE

Sarah's hands trembled as she folded and refolded the note. An eyelid began to twitch, and she fought the urge to run screaming through the neighborhood. Hurrying to the bathroom, she shook two pills from a prescription bottle and dry-swallowed them. She rummaged for another bottle, and a little white tablet followed the others down her throat. She ran scalding water and stretched out in the tub, gulping wine and waiting for the drugs to take effect. She startled awake when her chin splashed into the bathwater.

The medication and catnap cleared her head. Evan wasn't dead. His flight was missing. A simple glitch, according to the men at the airport. The plane would turn up, and Evan would come home. They would work things out. She dressed and ran a comb through her hair, then she drove across town to the airport. John Kelly didn't seem surprised to see her, as the burly man smiled and extended a hand.

Sarah wasted no time on niceties. "Any news?"

"It's just been a few hours, ma'am," he said in

an apologetic tone, "but we're making progress." He swiveled in his chair and pressed a clicker. "The highlighted region on this map represents an area of southern Washington. We've plotted the aircraft's flight path and last known location. Our technicians tell us the interruption in communication occurred over this area, narrowing down the plane's likely location."

Sarah tried to decipher the undulating mass of green covered with circles and lines, elevations, mountain ranges and lakes. Drawn in the middle was an enormous elongated shape. The area within it was barren, and there was nothing to indicate roads or towns. She couldn't imagine finding a small airplane in such a vast space.

"You really think it's in there?"

"That's our best guess. This is the aircraft's last verifiable location. Technicians are right now analyzing satellite images. Air search operations are underway. The National Guard and Civil Air Patrol are covering every inch of this grid. We've got ground rescue teams on alert and ready to go at a moment's notice."

"Don't airplanes have a signal that helps you find them? A black box, or whatever?"

"That's correct in most cases," he said. "All commercial aircraft use an electronic flight data recorder, the so-called black box. These devices tell us what went wrong, but they don't identify an airplane's location. Every large commercial passenger aircraft also carries an emergency locator system that's satellite tracked. They're rarely built into small aircraft like this one. We know the pilot of this flight was carrying a GPS locator device. We haven't been able to pick up the signal."

"Why not?"

Kelly chewed on a lip and seemed to think about what he wanted to say. "Two likely explanations come to mind. An aircraft experiences a sudden loss of cabin pressure, and everyone on board loses consciousness. If the plane is operating on autopilot, it continues on a certain course until the fuel is exhausted. Because the aircraft is under full power and not in an emergency circumstance, the system wouldn't activate."

"The other possibility?"

"A mid-air explosion disables emergency devices." Kelly raised a cautionary hand. "Ma'am, it's unlikely we're dealing with either of those situations."

Sarah fell silent. Staring at a meaningless map. Heart wanting to jump out of her chest. Trying to force air into her lungs. Fighting off the desire to scream at this man to get it over with and tell her Evan was dead. Pushing it all away. Forcing calm into her voice. "Any better scenarios?"

"Absolutely. A minor electronic malfunction or simple loss of cockpit communication could explain it."

"But you obviously don't think that happened," she

said. "You're looking for wreckage. In the middle of nowhere."

"Ma'am, that's just one aspect of the operation," Kelly said. "These are standard search procedures. We begin based on an aircraft's last known location. In this case, it's over a wilderness area. After we rule out that possibility, we move on to the next one. I'm certain we'll know something before the day's over."

He paused to shuffle through a stack of papers. "There was something I neglected to ask you this morning. Did you receive any communication from your husband last night? A phone call or text?"

"Why do you ask?"

"Passengers sometimes call loved ones in these situations."

"He didn't call or text," she said. "I want to know something, and I'd appreciate a straight answer. If this is one of those worst cases you mentioned, what are the chances someone could survive?"

"Better than you might think," Kelly said. "In nearly all aircraft mishaps, passengers survive the initial impact. For large commercial planes, there's about a ninety percent survival rate."

"Okay," she said slowly, "that's for a big aircraft. What about a little plane? Like the one my husband's on?"

"The odds aren't as good. Large commercial airplanes have higher survival rates for specific reasons. Most of the time, big airliners go down near a runway. There's plenty of open space, so they rarely crash into anything. Emergency crews are seconds away, and hospitals are close at hand. Most mishaps involve little more than a rough landing."

"It's different for planes like this one?"

"Smaller aircraft most often run into trouble in remote areas. Equipment is more likely to malfunction, engines fail at altitude, and pilots are less experienced in handling emergencies. They fly off course, and that makes them harder to locate. Small planes are less structurally sound than big jetliners. They don't go down near runways. They collide with trees or mountainsides and break apart. Passengers get thrown out or absorb greater impact. The few who survive are often in bad shape and lack any means of communication. They're usually in a remote area and it's harder for rescuers to find them."

Sarah felt heat rise to her face. She didn't want to hear about severe injuries or low odds. She wanted this man to give her some hope. To tell her Evan was coming home. She forced away the irritation and pressed on. "So, you're saying it's possible?"

"Miracles happen," Kelly said. "Sometimes it's plain luck. A passenger in one seat survives, the one beside him doesn't make it. Someone gets thrown clear and walks away with minor injuries. There've been instances when a plane clears a mountain peak by inches and goes down in a pasture. Everybody lives to tell the story. If the flight path were a foot lower, nobody survives. Then there's the human factor. Survival might depend on a person's physical condition or determination to live."

"My husband's in his forties," she said. "He's a child psychologist who sits in an office and talks to kids. He goes to a health club and lifts weights. He likes to jog, but he's not in the best of shape."

"Is he an outdoorsman?" Kelly asked. "Or a veteran?"

She shook her head. "But he grew up in the country and shot rabbits as a kid. We've gone camping a few times, and he might know a little about the outdoors. He was a Boy Scout, for what that's worth."

"What about his personality?"

"He's the most strong-willed man I've ever known. Evan's smart and resourceful. If anyone could figure out a way to survive something like this, it would be him."

Kelly glanced at his watch and escorted her out, promising to call with any new developments.

A woman sat in the waiting room. Short and stocky, she wore big glasses and an enormous cross around her neck. She clutched the cross as she dabbed at her eyes with a handkerchief. Sarah remembered her from last night. She approached and extended a hand.

"Sarah Winslow," she said. "You missing somebody, too?"

The woman offered a crooked smile and took her hand. "Rose Flanagan. My husband's co-pilot on the flight. Sixteen years he's flown, logging more than a thousand trips. Never an incident. Not even a close call." She rubbed a thumb across the giant cross. "Your husband on board?"

Sarah nodded. "I can't imagine why. He wasn't due home until Sunday."

Rose nodded towards the conference room. "Kelly have anything new?"

"Not really. He wanted to know if my husband called last night."

"My husband wouldn't have tried," Rose said, her voice quavering. "He'd have been busy doing his job and trying to protect the passengers."

As Sarah watched the woman fall to pieces, she felt her defenses begin to collapse. "This is the worst moment of my life," Rose whispered in a quavering voice. "I don't know what I'll do….."

She gulped for air and leaned into Sarah, sobbing on her shoulder. Sarah pulled the other woman close, feeling the wetness of Rose's tears. "Don't give up," she whispered. "They're coming home."

CHAPTER SIX

He rigged a solar compass by trimming a branch to a three-foot length and pushing it into the ground. Placing a small rock at the tip of the stick's shadow, he looked into the sky and estimated the sun's position. Using a sports watch borrowed from someone who would no longer need it, he set the timer to chime in three hours.

He returned to camp and sorted through gear. He loaded the backpack, slung the rifle onto a shoulder, and hoisted a sleeping bag onto the other. He attached the pistol and canteen to his belt. He took a test walk around the perimeter of the meadow and felt a jolt run up his back. He dumped the pack and started over.

He jettisoned the tent. Extra clothing and shoes. A camping stove. Shaving kit. Spare rifle and box of ammunition. He stuffed the rest into the pack and took another circuit around the meadow, and this time his back offered no objection. He decided to include a bourbon-filled canteen and a handful of cigars. Definite survival gear. He turned his attention to the meager food supply. A box of protein bars and a few tiny bags of peanuts. A couple of foil pouches of dehydrated food and a baggie filled with coffee.

The watch chimed.

He returned to the solar compass. The stick's shadow had moved a yard from the stone. He laid another rock at the tip of the shadow, dug a furrow between the two rocks, and drew a notch at the first shadow point. The result was a crudely drawn arrow pointing to the west. He had no idea how he possessed this knowledge, but he was confident it was correct. The arrow pointed towards a snow-capped mountain peak rising above the horizon.

Another nightfall. Another signal fire throwing flames into the night. He stretched out beside it and watched a panorama of constellations move across the sky. He poured a shot of whiskey and carried it through the darkness. He stopped in front of the line of shrouded bodies. Taking a strong pull of bourbon, he imagined himself lying among these men. His body stiff with rigor mortis. Forest animals feeding on him. He stared thoughtfully at his fellow castaways before returning to camp. He poked the fire and watched golden sparks jump into the darkness, then he settled in to sleep.

He awoke to the roar of engines and a rush of wind. The ground shook beneath his body. He raised an arm to shield his eyes from harsh yellow light shining down from the sky. A hand grasped his shoulder and shook him. In the distance, someone shouted his name and he heard a murmur of voices.

He startled awake.

The dream of rescue had been powerful and vivid. His chest was heaving, and he raised trembling hands to rub his face. He caressed the spot on his shoulder, where a hand had touched him. He tossed wood on the fire and waited until the flames were bright before again closing his eyes.

He rose early and made campfire coffee before attending to a final task. Rummaging through the backpack for the stack of ID's, he returned to the line of corpses. Stopping before each man, he read aloud each name and rendered an awkward salute.

He returned to camp and strapped on the backpack. He slung the rifle across his shoulder. At meadow's edge, he stopped for a last look at the line of bodies.

He walked into the wilderness.

The woods were postcard-perfect in the morning light. Crowded with tall conifers emitting a fragrant aroma, the forest floor was spongy with needles. Mountains rose in every direction. The sun warmed his face and chirping birds kept him in good spirits. As he marched along, the back loosened and his legs found a rhythm. He rested at midday, filling the canteen from a cold, clear stream.

By later afternoon, his body was beginning to

complain. He dropped the backpack beside another gurgling creek, slumped to the ground, and closed his eyes. An evening chill settled on his shoulders and awoke him. He gathered dead branches and lopped chunks of wood from a rotted log.

He filled the tin pot and set it on the flames, dumping boiling water into the contents of a shiny foil package. He didn't recognize the mushy mess, but it satisfied his hunger. He zipped himself into the sleeping bag and gazed at glittering stars. Feeling good. In control. Four miles closer to home.

He returned to the trail at daybreak and found easy passage through the forest. He passed time by attempting to fill in blank spots in his memory. He pulled out his driver's license and read it aloud. His name, address, and birth date. He noticed the organ donor designation. He rolled the plain gold band between finger and thumb and tried to recall his wife's name or face. He wondered if he had children.

Something pulled him from his reverie.

An odd sensation. The sense that he wasn't alone.

He turned to stare down the trail.

Nothing.

Minutes later, he felt it again.

The woods were silent. He again surveyed the trail behind him and saw nothing, but archetypal warning bells were screaming. Putting his body on full alert. Preparing it to run or fight, because something was coming his way. He scrambled up a sloping hill beside the deer trail. Unslinging the rifle, he dropped to the ground and waited.

He heard a rhythmic huffing.

A grizzly bear swayed down the trail. The animal was enormous. Looking the size of a Volkswagen. Nose to the ground. Following his scent. He recognized a splash of white on its flank. The grizzly from the crash site.

He brought the scope to his eye, training the crosshair on the bear's neck. The animal stopped below him, swiveling its massive head and gazing up the hillside. He stared into its depthless eyes and felt something ripple through his mind.

The bear remained motionless, wide brown eyes fixed on him. It abruptly turned and ambled down the hill. He watched the grizzly push through the underbrush and disappear into the woods.

He stared into the forest, trying to understand why a grizzly bear was following him. Wondering why it hadn't attacked him.

He slung the rifle onto a shoulder and returned to the trail.

CHAPTER SEVEN

Sarah spotted her friend in the darkened pub.

Sitting at a long mahogany bar and waving furiously, Marcie jumped up and ran to hug her. Sarah welcomed her friend's enthusiastic embrace. Marcie Malone was a real estate colleague, Sarah's gal pal and confidant, and the only person she was willing to meet in a bar at the worst moment of her life.

She sipped white wine while Marcie studied her face in a little mirror and dabbed at something with a pinky finger. Marcie was ten years younger and gloriously single. A tall blonde with a knockout body, her skirt scandalously short. She wore big glasses that gave her an adorable look. Her aura of innocence and radiating sexuality were irresistible, and Marcie was a major player in the dating scene.

Marcie demanded to be caught up on developments, which took all of a minute. Evan was still gone. The aircraft vanished into a million miles of wilderness. Government bureaucrats scratching their heads.

Insisting they were hot on the trail and but clueless about where to search for it.

"You look like a zombie," Marcie said. "You getting any sleep?"

"Not much. I feel worse than I look."

"Taking your meds?"

Sarah nodded. "Kicked up the dosage. It's helping a little."

"Good girl. But you need sleep. A couple of glasses of wine and an hour of useless chitchat should do the trick."

Marcie raised a manicured finger and the bartender hustled over with refills, then she launched into a litany of office politics and gossip. An agent was making big sales. Another unexpectedly pregnant. Promotions and firings. Big listings were rolling in, and Marcie was angling for them.

Shifting gears and moving on to her personal life, Marcie provided juicy details of a recent breakup. She was momentarily unattached, although Sarah knew from experience that status wouldn't last long. Marcie had a half-dozen eager candidates in mind. Sarah sipped wine and considered her friend's freewheeling lifestyle.

Hump 'em and dump 'em.

Marcie's motto. She owned a hot pink tee-shirt that flaunted the phrase across her abundant breasts.

A serial heartbreaker, Marcie changed relationships as often as thong underwear. Sarah suspected her friend enjoyed the thrill of the chase, as she impetuously cast aside lovers in pursuit of new ones.

Marcie abruptly stopped chattering. Her face had a somber look. "Have you talked to Nick?"

"No," she said, a bleak look on her face. "It doesn't matter anymore." She reached into her purse and handed the note to Marcie.

"Evan left this for me."

"Oh my God, sweetie." Marcie's eyes widened in surprise as she read it. "How'd he find out?"

"I don't know," Sarah said, misery and defeat evident in her voice. "Maybe he got into my texts. I'm such an idiot."

Marcie reached over to caress her friend's cheek. "Don't beat yourself up, honey. I know everything's horrible right now. But he'll come home, and you guys will fix things. Besides, weren't you going to tell him anyway?"

"Not this way. I wanted to explain it to him. Beg his forgiveness. Tell him I still love him. I broke his heart, Marcie. Lied to him. He got on that airplane because of my stupidity. This whole mess is my fault."

She sagged into her seat and rivulets of tears streamed down her face. Marcie moved close and hugged her. Then she pulled away and held Sarah at arm's length.

"Stop it, big baby," she said in a mock stern voice. "Don't be such a drama queen. You screwed up, honey. But that's life. Shit happens. We do stupid things. Now get over it. Evan still loves you. They'll find him. He'll come home, and you guys will work things out."

Sarah remembered they were in a bar. She was making a scene and people were looking her way. She released herself from Marcie's embrace.

"You're right," she said. "I need to stop blubbering." She picked up her glass and stared at the wine. "But I'm in living Hell, Marcie. I can't stop worrying about him. These horrible scenes keep running through my head. An airplane crashing. Evan hurt and bleeding. Lying there by himself. Helpless. Waiting for somebody to find him. And I'm sitting in a bar sucking down Chardonnay."

"Here's an idea," Marcie said. "How about getting off your butt and doing something about it?"

Sarah turned to look into her friend's face. "Like what?"

"Why don't you look for him."

"Great idea," Sarah said. "I'll skydive into the wilderness first thing in the morning. I'll drop into the woods and get on his trail. I'll take along some bloodhounds. The entire United States government can't find him, but by God, I can."

"Smartass," Marcie said. "I'm serious. You said the government has a search operation underway,"

Marcie said. "They must have set up a headquarters. You know where they're located?"

"Seattle, I think."

"Then get your ass up to Seattle."

"And do what?"

"Get in their business," Marcie said. "Find out what these people are doing. Where they're looking. Be a total pain in their asses. You'll feel better, and it might motivate them. If my man were lost in the wilderness, my rear end would be on the next flight to Seattle."

"I don't know," Sarah said.

"Don't be such a wuss. Book a flight to Seattle and raise some hell. Park yourself in their command center. Bug the hell out of them."

Sarah stared into her wine glass.

"What if you were lost? What would Evan do?"

"Look for me. Never stop until he found me."

Marcie cocked a brow and said nothing.

"You've always been a great closer," Sarah conceded. "You made your sale. I'll go to Seattle."

"Great idea," Marcie replied with a smile. "I'm going with you."

CHAPTER EIGHT

Following a bumpy three-hour flight from Phoenix, they dropped through billowing cloud banks and spotted Seattle's jagged skyline. Marcie elbowed her and pointed towards the silhouette of the Space Needle. Its distinctive saucer-shaped halo jutted high into the overcast sky and slowly rotated. The plane dropped onto a rain-slicked runway and they walked through the gangway into the Sea-Tac Airport.

The hyperactive Marcie had handled everything. She'd rushed home after happy hour and booked their flight, found a hotel room and rented a car. She'd conducted a Google search and found the name of the FAA representative in charge of the investigation. She made calls to the Seattle airport and strong-armed someone into giving her the man's number, then she called him to arrange a meeting. Marcie next contacted a local charter company and arranged for a small plane to fly them over the search area. She even picked up Sarah in Scottsdale and chauffeured her to the airport.

They checked into a commuter hotel located next

to Sea-Tac, and over dinner and wine brainstormed questions to ask the FAA representative. Sarah typed them into her phone, so she'd remember them in the morning. They returned to their room with a bottle of wine. Sarah rummaged through her purse for the medicine bottle, shook out two pills and chased them with a sip of wine, then she fell asleep to the drumming of Seattle's ever-present rain.

In the morning, they followed directions to an administrative wing in the main airport terminal. A friendly administrative person deposited them in a sparsely furnished office, where they were greeted by an FAA representative named Springer. He had the look of a new-age bureaucrat. Young and sharply dressed, the man's short razor-cut hair gave him the appearance of an investment banker.

They sat across from his desk while Springer provided an overview of the hunt for Air Pacific Flight 272. He explained that search operations were handled by a command center located at an airbase in western Florida. Springer's job was to coordinate the various agencies involved in the search.

He led them through a briefing that included maps, charts, flyover photos of the search area, and a list of organizations participating in the search. He followed up with a series of satellite images. Springer explained the heat sensing technology utilized by the military search planes. The man assured them that finding the Air Pacific flight was the FAA's top priority and the search and rescue operation was top-notch and professionally managed. When he finished his spiel, he smiled at the women and asked for questions.

Sarah scrolled through her phone, studying her list, then she focused her gaze on Springer. "We appreciate you taking the time to see us and explain all this," she said. "It's good to know so many are looking for my husband. But you didn't say anything about the progress of your search. Where do things stand?"

"Ma'am, first let me say that over the past seventy-two hours we've conducted the most extensive aerial search operation ever undertaken in the northwest," he said. "Dozens of aircraft have conducted hundreds of low- and high-level overflights. Our technicians have reviewed hours of air traffic communications. They've studied satellite pictures in great detail. We've even interviewed pilots who were flying in the proximity of the mishap. We're using all available technology."

"We get it," Sarah said. She was growing impatient with Springer, who was now parroting what he already told them. "Your search is vast and comprehensive. You're doing all kinds of things. You have planes in the air and people studying pictures. But what has all this searching produced?"

"Honestly," Springer said, "not much."

Sarah felt heat rise to her face. "We flew fifteen

hundred miles for 'not much?' How is it possible that an airplane could simply vanish?"

Springer's façade of confidence had fallen away and his face was now flushed as he tugged nervously at his tie. "We're closing in on an answer," he said. "We've learned quite a bit about what happened the evening of the mishap."

"Okay," she said. "What do you know?"

"Following the flight's takeoff that evening," Springer said, "a loss of communication occurred between the control tower and the Air Pacific pilot. This was a critical event because it occurred just when the Seattle tower handed the aircraft over to Salt Lake air traffic control."

Sarah's foot was tapping the floor with growing intensity, a sure-fire barometer of her accelerating anxiety. Marcie reached over and gently pressed on her friend's thigh until the tapping stopped.

"As I said, this was a critical incident," Springer continued. "Message logs show the controller did his part during the handover. He communicated with the aircraft and advised the pilot to contact Salt Lake's air control tower. That's standard procedure. But there's no indication the pilot responded or contacted Salt Lake air traffic control."

"Is that unusual?"

"It's rare," Springer said, "but it happens. Sometimes pilots don't acknowledge when controllers hand them off. Flight crews have a lot to occupy them during takeoff and landing. At times they neglect to notify approach controllers when they're entering their air space, or the controller's too busy to wait for an answer. Most of the time, it's unimportant. In this case, it was a significant event."

"Why so important?"

"Well, ma'am, this communication failure meant no control center was tracking the aircraft for nearly three hours after the handoff. The plane could have flown in any direction or landed anywhere. It's increased our search area exponentially, although we have narrowed down the possibilities."

Marcie waved her hand like she was still in high school and offered Springer a brilliant smile. "Where is the search area, and how big is it?"

Sarah watched as Springer ran his eyes over Marcie's splendid legs and dangerously short skirt. He was a young man and Sarah recognized the look in his eye. Marcie was major league talent, and Sarah suspected X-rated images of her friend were running through Springer's mind. Springer offered Marcie a hopeful smile as he clicked a map onto the screen. He tapped a pointer onto a large area circled in red.

"We're certain the plane disappeared in this region," he said, "which encompasses six thousand square miles. That's a lot of area to cover. It's difficult for search planes to spot anything from the air and practically impossible to conduct a ground search. The remoteness of the area itself further complicates things. There are no roads or marked trails in this region. It's nearly inaccessible."

Sarah stared at the map, wanting to scream in frustration. Evan was lost in some horrible place, injured or dying. Meanwhile, this government bureaucrat glibly rambled on with his useless briefing. As she listened to Springer spout his crap, she fought off the urge to jump across the table and shake him.

"I want to go along tomorrow," she said. "In one of the search planes."

Springer tapped into a laptop and studied the screen. "That may not be possible."

"Why not?"

"The search has been drawn down."

He raised his hands and offered an apologetic smile. "I know it's not what you want to hear, but it's literally out of my hands. The team commander down in Florida's the final authority. He determines the location and duration of the search. He allocates resources. The search is most intense the first few days, then it's drawn down. Yesterday, the search commander scaled back operations."

"They stopped looking for him?"

"No, ma'am. Fewer resources are now allocated, and the search is coordinated on a local level, by Civil Air Patrol commanders."

"How many airplanes?"

Springer again consulted his laptop. "I'm looking at the CAP website," he said. He shrugged and gave her the same sorrowful look.

"One mission yesterday. None scheduled today."

"Tomorrow? The next day?"

"I'm sorry, ma'am," he said. "The next mission won't commence until the weekend."

Sarah felt herself shrinking, growing distant from the world. Springer seemed far away, his voice echoing through her head. She wondered if she was going to faint. Marcie took her arm and guided her from the room and through the terminal. People flowed past, but she felt disconnected from them. At the hotel, Sarah fell onto the bed and allowed her emotions their release.

"They've stopped looking, Marcie," she cried. "They've abandoned him."

Marcie lay on the bed and put her arms around Sarah. She murmured consoling words, stroking her hair as if Sarah were a child. Marcie uncorked a bottle and poured wine into a tumbler, then she walked to the window and stared at the cloud-shrouded mountain range.

"Screw the government," she said. "Screw Springer and the horse he rode in on. We'll find Evan ourselves."

Sarah raised her head and looked at Marcie. "We will?"

"Damn right," Marcie said. "Tomorrow morning."

CHAPTER NINE

The next morning, they got into the rental and Marcie punched an address into her phone. She directed Sarah to the freeway, and they fought rush hour traffic while traveling west towards Seattle. They exited on Marcie's command stopped at the entrance for Boeing Field. This was a much smaller airfield than Sea-Tac, although a row of passenger aircraft was parked along its main runway. A bevy of smaller planes circled above the field. They drove towards the far end of the main runway, towards an area filled with hangars. Aircraft of varying sizes sat in front of open bay doors.

"This used to be Seattle's main airport until they built Sea-Tac." Marcie was reading from her phone. "Nowadays, they use it as a regional airport for air taxis and smaller aircraft, but mostly Boeing builds and tests airplanes here." They continued along a little road running behind the hangars until Marcie pointed to the one they wanted.

The ancient galvanized steel Quonset hut was of World War II vintage. Decades ago, the hut was painted red, although the years had oxidized it to rust. End walls of the semi-circular building were framed with desiccated plywood that was peeling paint. An old door hung at an angle and was outfitted with an ancient porcelain knob. The sign above the door looked newer. ***Rainier Charter Tours***.

They entered through the crooked door, footsteps echoing on the concrete floor as they stepped into the hangar. Parked in the middle of the building was a vintage biplane. It might have been from the Wright Brothers era, although the paint was bright and new.

A man was leaning into the engine compartment, turning something with a wrench. He turned and wiped his hands at their approach. He was young and sandy-haired, wearing dirty mechanics coveralls.

"Cute," Marcie whispered as he approached.

"You must be Sarah and Marcie." He grinned and stuck out a hand. "I'm Mike McLean, your tour guide for the day."

Marcie was looking skeptically at the airplane. "You're not serious?"

McLean laughed and thumped the side of the plane. "You're in the presence of aircraft royalty," he said. "The Sopwith Camel. This beauty's a hundred years old and still running like a top. It's legendary. The premier dogfighting aircraft in World War I, and the airplane Snoopy used to shoot down the mighty Red Baron."

He provided them an engaging smile. "This aircraft's safer than you might think. Most of the body is original. Everything else is brand new. I rebuilt the engine last year and replaced every mechanical component with modern parts. Flying in this baby's the closest thing to heaven you'll ever experience."

"Nope." Marcie shook her head and turned to Sarah. "I'm not going anywhere in that thing," she said. Sarah was gazing doubtfully at the ancient aircraft. She nodded in agreement, and they turned to leave.

"This isn't your ride, ladies," McLean called after them. He flashed another smile. "Besides, it's only got one seat." He motioned for them to follow. The man slid open the hangar doors and led them onto an arterial taxiway connected to the main runway. McLean pointed to a larger and newer aircraft.

"This is our transportation for the day," he said. "A Cessna 172 Sky Hawk. Sweetest running and safest little plane in the sky. I bought this last year, and she's logged less than a hundred flying hours. She's got a range of 800 miles, so she can easily take you where you want to go." He offered them another flirtatious smile. "You'll love flying in it."

He led them into a cubicle where they signed a stack of papers and handed over a thousand dollars for four hours of flight time. McLean moved to a big area map pinned to the wall. He picked up a pencil and drew a long oval on the map.

"Like I mentioned when you called, I fly with the Civil Air Patrol and took part in the initial search for Air Pacific 272. Our friend Springer probably told you this circled area represents the region where your husband's most likely gonna be found. Once we get in the air, I'll do a high-altitude flyover to give you an idea of the scope of the area. We'll spend the rest of the time looking for your guy."

He loaded them onto the Cessna and fired it up, and a few minutes later they were taxiing onto the runway. After a smooth liftoff, they angled into the sky and soon were flying high above the earth. McLean handed them headphones and pointed out various sights as they rose to ten thousand feet.

"My God," Marcie said.

She was staring slack-jawed at the majestic peak of Mount Rainier.

The immense mountain towered above them like a mystical apparition and seemed to be floating in a bed of billowing clouds. The mountain's slopes were covered in blue-tinged glacial ice that sparkled and reflected the sun's rays. They saw wisps of smoke emerging from the mountain's peak.

"Fire and ice," McLean narrated. "The most amazing mountain in the world and the most beautiful sight I've ever seen. The Native Americans call it Tacoma and once believed a lake of fire burned on its summit. According to their legends, monsters and spirits lived up there, so they never climbed it. I can understand why they considered the mountain a magical place. Rainier is still an active volcano, yet it's covered year-round in snow and glacial ice. It never fails to awe me." McLean made his living flying tourists to Mount Rainier, and he was dispensing his well-rehearsed travel guide pitch.

"Mount Rainier rises more than fourteen thousand feet into the sky," he continued. "Burning gases and molten rock are constantly flowing inside the mountain, yet it's been covered for thousands of years with snow and ice. The melting water feeds the rivers and streams you see down below. Rainier stands so tall that it actually traps clouds and keeps them from moving on, and the rainfall creates all the greenery you see down there. The natives believe Rainier is the spirit mountain that creates life, but it also has a nasty side. The last major eruption occurred in 1890, although there are still tremblers. The problems with this mountain aren't volcanic. Snowmelt's the issue. There's a constant flow of water that triggers dozens of major mudslides every year."

Finished with his travelogue, McLean shut up and allowed them to stare in silence at the majestic mountain as it slid past. The pilot banked to the west and pointed towards a string of smaller volcanic mountains.

"These are the Cascades," he said into the mike.

"They run from Canada to California. Eons ago, when glaciers pushed aside the earth and created these mountains, they left behind a string of valleys and glacial lakes. It's the most fertile ground on the planet. That big snow-covered mountain in the distance is Mount Hood. It's seventy miles from here."

McLean unfolded a map and put it on Sarah's lap.

"I want to give you some idea of the problem," he said. "The government experts think the airplane disappeared in this area between Rainier and Hood. If it made contact with either of those mountains, we might never find it because the higher slopes are impassible. If the plane missed the mountains, there's a million square miles of forest and hundreds of valleys where it might be hiding."

He reached over to tap the map. "You also have to think about the lakes. There must be hundreds of them down there. It could be sitting on the bottom of one. The search team did their best, but in truth they probably covered ten percent of the search area from the air. They won't put boots on ground until they find something." McLean rummaged in a console and produced binoculars, which he handed to Sarah.

She leaned her forehead against the cold window and stared down at the landscape. An endless expanse of green carpet stretched in every direction, giving the appearance of an infinite emerald ocean. She realized she was looking at the tops of millions of densely packed trees, their branches overlapping to conceal anything on the ground.

She used the binoculars to scan the landscape. Even with the glasses, it was impossible to see beneath the treetops. With sinking spirits, she understood why the air search team hadn't found the plane and saw the impossibility of a ground search.

A flash of something caught her eye, a glint or reflection from outside the port window emanating miles from their location. She called out and pointed an arm, and McLean swung the plane around.

"Might have been the sun glinting off a lake," he said, "but let's take a look." He dropped the plane into a valley and skimmed treetops until climbing back to altitude.

Sarah was staring towards the distant mountain. "Does it look like this all the way to Mount Hood?"

"Pretty much."

"If someone was down there, could they walk out?"

"It would be tough," McLean said.

"How far would they have to go?"

"Depends on the direction," he said. "At this latitude, there's nothing to the east for hundreds of miles. You wouldn't go north or south because of the topography. To hike out, you'd have to travel west. You'd run into civilization within a couple of hundred miles. I've hiked in those woods a few times, and it's no walk in the park. It's easy to lose your bearings down there. The forest is dense, and you can't see fifty feet in front of you. It's hard to figure out your direction."

He continued the flight to Mount Hood before making a turn and dropping to a lower altitude. McLean began zigzagging across the search area while Sarah and then Marcie stared through the binoculars. After a while, they put down the glasses.

Sarah gazed out the window at the vast wilderness.

"Take us back," she said.

CHAPTER TEN

He shaded his eyes and squinted into the sky.

The droning echoed across the valley, and he caught a speck of movement against the mountain's backdrop. He raised the binoculars and spotted the small aircraft. Roughly a mile from his location, skimming the treetops. As the plane banked and made another pass, he pulled out the shaving mirror and raised it skyward. Trying to reflect sunlight towards the plane. The aircraft continued to move away and disappeared into the horizon.

He lit a fire and threw on green branches to get it smoking. He sat cross-legged and stared at the sky, shaving mirror at the ready. When the fire died out, he returned to the trail. After a strong afternoon of hiking, he set up camp near a fast-flowing creek. He dipped in the canteen and enjoyed the taste of icy glacier water. He pulled the remaining foil pouch from his backpack and started the evening fire.

A big jackrabbit with enormous ears hopped into view at the forest's edge. The animal stopped to nibble at the coarse turf, its body turned in profile. He raised the rifle and sighted, took a deep breath, and pulled the trigger. The kick of the weapon knocked him onto his backside. He let out a victory whoop when discovering the slug had torn through the rabbit's body. He hacked at it with the hunting knife, salvaging back legs and haunches. He relished the meager meal, during which he discovered that rabbit tasted nothing like chicken.

After a week on the trail, days and evenings fell into a routine. He marked his direction each morning using the solar compass to identify a distant landmark. Although the desired route sometimes required him to push his way through heavy underbrush, he tried to follow game trails. He kept a close watch for the grizzly. Late each afternoon, he pitched camp near running water and kept a fire burning all night on the chance an aircraft might spot it. The landscape gradually transitioned as he moved further westward, becoming hilly and dense with vegetation.

He had miscalculated in estimating his ability to cover ground. He was hiking less than three miles a day, insufficient to escape the wilderness before winter's arrival. He needed to cover at least four miles, but injuries and pain were restricting his progress. He decided to push harder in the coming days.

He made camp on a hillside above an elongated valley. After gathering wood and setting the fire ablaze, he tore open the last food packet and dumped it into a cup of hot water. The aroma of beef stew emanated from the mush, and he slowly consumed every morsel. He rinsed the cup and drank the watery broth.

Sunlight remained in the day, so he climbed to a higher elevation and surveyed the valley he would traverse tomorrow. Nature had carved a narrow rift in the earth and shaped it into a lush breadbasket. He guessed the valley spanned fifty miles across. Running down its midsection was a winding river that sparkled in the late-day sun. An evening mist rose from the rift, and he watched fog form on the valley floor, giving the place a wild and primordial appearance. The ground was dense with foliage. He estimated he would require ten days to traverse it.

He ran his eyes across the landscape. The jagged mountain ranges linked together like a string of jade pearls. He spotted no sign of human habitation. No city lights or ribbons of highway, no malls, restaurants or hospitals. No smoke from distant fires. Only an endless ocean of foliage and a string of white-capped mountains. The valley before him gave the appearance of a faraway planet. He was a solitary astronaut marooned on it.

He rolled into the sleeping bag and stared at a nighttime panorama so brilliant it appeared artificial. He spotted blinking aircraft lights miles above him and heard engine sounds echoing from the sky. A passenger aircraft outbound from Seattle, he guessed, settling into cruising altitude. Passengers would be reclining their seats and ordering meals and drinks. They would enjoy the inflight movie as they passed overhead, oblivious to his presence. He watched the winking lights until they disappeared and fell asleep contemplating the ghostly swath of the Milky Way.

He opened his eyes and the face of an angel hovered above his head. Her body backlit by soft light. A shimmering corona surrounded her head. He strained to bring her face into focus, feeling a pang of recognition. She gazed down at him with a sad smile, whispering words he couldn't hear. She drifted closer and placed soft lips against his cheek, emanating a fragrance that filled his senses.

He awoke from the dream and for a moment her image floated holographically overhead before dissolving into the night. He touched his cheek where her lips had touched it. He stared into the darkness, trying to understand a dream that didn't feel like one. He remained awake for a long time, trying to identify what was unsettling about the hovering angel and her soft kiss.

He began his gradual descent into the ancient valley. The day was sparkling and fresh, exactly like the one before it. The sky was blue and the weather warm. The trees were painted a vivid green, and the forest resonated with bird songs. He felt his spirits rise as he made easy passage through the woods.

He entered an expanse of aspen and stopped to sniff the air, inhaling a subtle aroma drifting in with the wind. Exotic and familiar, the fragrance triggered a recollection of the angel from last night's dream. Her opaque image floated through his mind, and he felt a vague sense of recognition. It danced just beyond the outskirts of his memory.

He kept a good pace as he descended into the valley. Perspiration formed on his neck as the day grew warmer, and after a morning of hiking he arrived at the edge of the river. Its roar filled his ears as he marveled at nature's power and perfection. Blue-green waters birthed by glacial runoff sparkled in the morning sun and cut a winding path through the heart of the valley. The current ran wide and shallow, crashing into enormous rocks and forming foamy rapids. Fast and purposeful, the water threw off energy and possibility.

He tossed rocks into the current and gave thought to building a raft. It would require him to fell big trees and trim them into logs. Strong binding would be necessary to withstand the river's strong currents.

The only cutting tools he possessed were hooked to his belt. The hatchet and hunting knife. It would take weeks to chop and trim enough logs. Even if he managed that improbable feat, he had nothing to bind them beyond a small length of nylon rope. The raft would weigh hundreds of pounds. How would he push it into the water? How might he steer it? He threw a stick into the river and watched it bob away, carrying with it the fantasy of floating home. He resumed walking along the bank until the river bent north, then he turned into the forest.

He made camp in late afternoon. His food supply nearly gone, he spent a fruitless two hours hunting. Dinner consisted of airline peanuts and a bit of rabbit flesh. He banked the fire and fell asleep atop his bedroll.

A hooting owl awoke him.

He threw a chunk of wood on the embers, uncapped the canteen, and poured bourbon into a tin cup. He grimaced at the liquor's strong taste while watching yellow flames jump and dance against the night's backdrop. He rummaged through the pack until locating the shaving mirror. He held it up to the light.

He stared at a face he did not recognize. A life forgotten. He attempted to visualize his wife's face. To remember what he did for a living. What made him laugh. His dreams and ambitions. Why he was on an airplane. A rustling noise interrupted his reverie. He cocked his head and listened. A tiny crackling sound, perhaps a breaking branch. He peered into the dark forest and detected a subtle shifting of shadows beyond the tree line.

A figure stood beneath the canopy of a tree.

Silently swaying in a rhythmic way. Phosphorescent eyes staring at him. The sight unleashed a panoply of vivid imaginings that instantly transformed him from a grown man into a wide-eyed child shivering in a dark bedroom. Hiding beneath the covers, trembling in fear. A hideous creature lurked in the closet or beneath his bed. A monster or goblin. The bogeyman. A vampire.

He shook his head to clear long-forgotten childhood fears. Raising the rifle, he curled a finger around the trigger and tried to interpret what he was seeing. Something was definitely there. Standing too tall and broad for a human being. The grizzly came to mind, but he dismissed the idea. The bear that followed him crashed through the woods like a laboring freight train. He couldn't imagine what other forest animal would cast such an odd shadow. He watched as the shape began to shimmer, then it was gone. He flipped on the flashlight and ran it around the tree line, wondering if his mind was playing tricks on him.

He kept the fire burning brightly that night and fell asleep clutching the rifle.

CHAPTER ELEVEN

Sarah sat cross-legged in the dark closet, clutching a baggie of pills and thinking about a chocolate Lab named Buster. On the second Christmas of their marriage, Evan surprised her with the wriggling puppy. Buster became their surrogate child and took over the house. They pampered the pooch, feeding him treats, allowing him to jump on furniture and providing an endless supply of toys. Buster had a fondness for tennis balls, leaping in ecstasy at the sight of one.

She sipped whiskey from a water glass while remembering how Buster reacted when given a new ball. He would prance about the house holding it in his mouth, showing off his treasure to everyone. Scattering furniture as he chased after it. After about a week, he seemed to lose interest in the thing. Buster would eventually set to work tearing the ball to shreds, hell-bent on destroying the thing he valued most in the world.

Sarah turned her attention to the plastic baggie. She ran her fingers over the contents, caressing the tiny pills with fingertips. There were six of them. Each one a robin-egg blue. A miniature heart carved in the middle. Dumped last night from her prescription bottle into the baggie. She'd detoured into Evan's study to pick up the whiskey bottle before crawling into the closet.

She remembered the day her descent into Hell began.

It started a year ago. She awoke one sunny July morning and felt a pulse of energy bounce through her body. Not usually a morning person, she bounded out of bed on this one and raced through her day like a hyperactive teenager. Days later, the same thing happened again. She woke up early and felt the electrical current humming through her body like sugar buzz. She rode the wave through a busy day of selling property. These juiced days became more frequent, and she began anticipating them. She never ran out of energy, showing homes from dawn to dusk and juggling a dozen balls without dropping one.

Her emotions became wilder, and her behavior hyperactive. She couldn't sit still, talked too fast, and laughed too loud. She began fighting urges to dance at the most inappropriate times. Then came the intense and urgent sexual desires. She started wanting to do risky things, like having sex in the car. Evan noticed and happily complied, once jokingly suggesting she cut down on caffeine.

One morning, she awoke with a different feeling. The sun streamed through the window, but she felt listless. Her body ached like the flu, and she wondered if she might be coming down with something. She canceled her schedule, drew the drapes, and slept away the day. The funk lasted three days before the pulse of energy returned. She welcomed its arrival, jumping from bed and racing off to work.

Deciding it was time for new shoes, one morning she dashed to the big mall on Camelback Road and bought a pair of Louis Vuitton stiletto heels. Hurrying past a Cartier's, she spotted a glittering bracelet. She ran inside and bought the thing, paying no mind to the twelve-thousand-dollar price tag. Two days later, she couldn't imagine what motivated her to spend so recklessly. She returned the bracelet, shredding the receipt and never telling Evan. Then she dashed into a dealership and drove away in a hundred-thousand-dollar Mercedes convertible. Evan said little, although she knew he was not pleased with her behavior. After a few days, she humiliatingly returned the car.

Her moods gradually spiraled out of control. She blew up on a client who quibbled before signing off on a million-dollar property. A simple concession would have cost her a hundred dollars, but she became irritated and said something insulting. The client walked away from the sale, and she blamed him for being unreasonable. She began to suspect rival realtors were plotting to steal her clients. One afternoon, she had an ugly scene with an agent showing a house she had listed.

Coworkers began moving cautiously around her, and eventually her boss called her in for a performance review. In no mood for a lecture, Sarah stormed out and drove away stewing in anger. She rear-ended another vehicle and blamed the other driver, erupting in fury when the officer handed her the citation. She drove home recklessly and stormed into the house, ranting about the unfairness of it.

Evan calmly listened until she finished, then pulled her into his arms. Sarah's walls collapsed, and she began crying into his chest.

"Something's wrong with me," she whispered. "I don't know what it is."

"I think I do," he said.

She didn't argue when Evan made an appointment with a psychiatrist and within days felt better as the medication took effect. She learned to use calming strategies and enrolled in a yoga class. She discovered the meditative qualities of gardening and began growing roses in the back yard.

She hadn't yet engaged in her final act of stupidity.

Feeling better, she began to wonder if she needed the medication. She missed the adrenaline rushes and the energy and creativity they provided. The highs were wild and exhilarating carnival rides. Everyday life felt tedious and monotonous. One day she stopped taking the medicine. Flushed the pills down the toilet and lied to Evan. A few days later, the craziness returned.

She'd been partnering with an agent named Nick Watson. A few years younger and single, Nick was extremely good looking. They made high dollar sales and celebrated with expensive dinners. Sarah became preoccupied with him and began imagining them in bed. She started dressing provocatively and changed her hair color. Nick noticed her attention and returned it. She began sending him sex-charged texts, including a string of embarrassing selfies. Eventually, they stepped over the line.

Then Evan's plane disappeared, and she read his note.

Her world came crashing down. She'd cheated on the man she loved. Lied to him. Hurt him so badly that he couldn't be near her. She was the reason he boarded that plane. It was her fault he was missing and maybe dead. She plunged into the darkest place she had ever known. All she could think of was Evan. All she wanted to do was talk to him. Explain things. Beg his forgiveness. But that would never happen. He was gone. The disastrous trip to Seattle crushed any hope that she could salvage their marriage. Nobody was looking for him. He wasn't coming home.

She shook out a handful of pills.

She stared at them for a long time, then she tossed the pills down her throat.

She lay down in the dark closet and waited to die.

CHAPTER TWELVE

Bob Childress stared into the computer screen, chewing a lip as he studied the high-altitude picture. He manipulated the mouse and zoomed in tight, focusing his attention on a hundred-square-yard section of forest. He ran sharp eyes over the photo - top to bottom, then left to right - looking for anything unnatural or out of place. He discarded the image and brought the next one on-screen.

The sequence of satellite pictures encompassed a four-mile wide strip of terrain running Oregon's length, each image covering a square mile of forest. The pictures were digital and of perfect clarity, and his computer allowed him to enlarge each one a thousand times, to the point of seeing insects crawling on the ground.

Childress was searching for Air Pacific flight 272.

In ten years of controlling commercial aircraft, he'd never lost a plane until this one disappeared in front of his face. He'd cleared the flight for takeoff and sent it into the air. The missing aircraft gnawed at him. His logical mind knew it wasn't his fault, but that didn't stop him from feeling responsible.

Childress was familiar with search operation procedures and was confident they had been followed. The agency responsible for managing aircraft search and rescue operations was the Air Force Rescue Coordination Center, the AFRCC, located on Tyndall Air Base in Florida. On alert status around the clock, the command center immediately responded to the FAA advisory confirming the disappearance of Air Pacific flight 272.

The on-duty commander ordered his team to collect information, including the aircraft's departure time, last known location, route, airspeed, bearing, and passenger manifest. Technicians searched for an electronic trail, accessing military and civilian satellite systems to determine if the pilot activated the plane's emergency locator. Other technicians checked weather and climate conditions, which they fed into a mainframe. The computer ran its algorithm and calculated a search radius.

Ninety minutes after the FAA alert, the search mission went operational.

A bevy of aircraft took flight and began a systematic pattern of flyovers. Most of these planes were owned by members of the Civil Air Patrol and piloted by volunteers. The commander of the guard base in Portland deployed a half-dozen Sikorsky Pave

Hawk choppers. A total of thirty-six aircraft flew nonstop missions from dawn to dusk. This included a night operation, with pilots and spotters scanning the darkness for lights or flares.

Meanwhile, command center coordinators at Tyndall pored over maps and satellite imagery. The aircraft's estimated flight path skirted the western edge of the Cascades, an enormous mountain range extending across the northwest United States and into Canada. A vast wilderness area lay on this latitude, filling the space between the Cascades and the Pacific Ocean. The region was completely uninhabited, with some areas so remote they were considered unexplored. A network of rugged gorges and high mountains added to the difficulty of the operation.

The AFRCC mainframe calculated to a 99% probability that the aircraft disappeared within this region. The team commander ruled out a ground search. Even if searchers pinpointed a crash site, getting a rescue team on the ground was logistically difficult, if not impossible. It proved a moot point, because three days of intensive air searching turned up no sign of the missing plane.

Seventy-two hours after commencement, the team commander issued a downgrade in the operation's priority. From experience, he knew they were no longer engaged in a rescue mission. They were now searching for bodies. After another day of overflights, the Civil Air Patrol volunteers went home and parked their airplanes. The Portland air guard commander stood down his choppers. A small passenger craft went down in the mountains of northern Montana. The AFRCC commander shut down the search for Flight 272 and diverted resources to the more urgent operation.

Childress had closely monitored every step. The decision to call off the search was simple protocol and consistent with search and rescue triage. The most exigent situation received AFRCC time and resources. Another air crash had occurred, and it was now the focus of attention. Childress concurred with the team commander's conclusion regarding the unlikelihood of finding the aircraft.

He wasn't answerable for the missing plane, but he couldn't stop thinking about it. The *what-ifs* ran relentlessly through his head. What if he'd paid more attention to the little commuter plane? Should he have kept his eyes on the screen longer? Should he have waited for a response from the aircraft pilot?

The same day the AFRCC shut down its operation, Childress began his unofficial search for Air Pacific Flight 272. He was single and had nothing to distract him beyond a grumpy cat named Felix. Every night after his shift at Sea-Tac, Childress returned to his apartment and turned on an iMac desktop. He started by studying the computerized record of the plane's flight. He had cleared the aircraft for takeoff at 10:20 p.m. on a Saturday. Shortly afterward, it lifted uneventfully into the air. Weather conditions were clear and warm. Thirty-four minutes later, at 10:54 p.m., the flight left Seattle airspace and Childress wished the pilot a safe journey. Despite hearing no response from the pilot, Childress relinquished control of the aircraft. Its digital footprint should have popped up on Salt Lake's screens.

That's where things went haywire.

Somewhere between Seattle and Salt Lake, electronic monitoring was lost and there was no verification the plane entered Salt Lake's air space. The aircraft pilot didn't contact the Salt Lake tower, and the flight wasn't picked up an hour later by controllers in Eugene, 120 miles to the south. A computer-generated advisory was issued, notifying every control tower on the west coast to look for the plane on their grids.

Childress went line-by-line over the AFRCC report and decided to run the numbers for himself. He loaded the plane's airspeed, bearing, and altitude into a program run by the mainframes at Sea-Tac. He inputted the pilot's flight plan and the aircraft's last known location. Its algorithm calculated the plane's most likely landing point, and the result was similar to the one generated by the AFRCC in Florida. The aircraft vanished somewhere in a three-hundred-mile area between Seattle and Eugene. The AFRCC's computers had provided a search area extending ten miles on each side of the aircraft's route, resulting in a grid encompassing six thousand square miles. Childress could understand why the search operation failed. A needle in a haystack would be easier to locate.

He leaned back in his chair and closed his eyes, reviewing the facts at hand. The aircraft had followed a standard flight path from Seattle to San Francisco, known to controllers as Air Route 93. A commonly used highway in the sky. No problems were reported on takeoff. The pilot issued no call for assistance. The craft's onboard computers transmitted no electronic communication. The aircraft's emergency locator signal was never activated. All this information led to one inescapable conclusion.

The plane went down instantly.

Two possibilities came to his mind. The plane exploded in flight or experienced a catastrophic loss of power. In either circumstance, the aircraft would have plunged to the ground without time to veer from its route. Childress decided to reduce the search parameters. He instructed the computer to calculate a grid two miles on either side of the plane's flight path, instead of ten miles as the AFRCC had used. This resulted in a twelve-hundred square mile search area. A large chunk of landscape, but far more manageable.

Felix padded into the room and jumped on his lap. Childress petted the cat as it mewled, then he figured out what it wanted. He got up and opened the front door. The cat went outside to take care of its business. Childress yawned and stretched, looking at his watch. It was 3:30 a.m., and his eyes were burning. The folks at Tyndall had sent him a file of satellite photos covering the aircraft's flight path between Seattle and Eugene. The file consisted of twelve hundred pictures, each covering a square mile. Childress had spent the past three nights segmenting and enlarging each image.

He went into the kitchen and poured a cup of stale coffee. Grimacing as he sipped the bitter brew, he returned to the computer and magnified another photo. All were numbingly similar, containing little more than snapshots of treetops and brown earth. An occasional bear or deer interrupted the boredom. He worked his way through two dozen images, studying each one before moving it to the trash bin.

He heard a meowing and went to the door to let in Felix. The cat disappeared into the apartment and Childress returned to the study. He was deciding whether to turn off the computer when a flash of color caught his eye.

Something rectangular and painted white, with a slash of red. Not the shape or color of things typically found in the forest. Childress enlarged the picture and fiddled with focus.

Despite the hour, he picked up the phone and called Tyndall.

CHAPTER THIRTEEN

The deer stepped through dappled sunlight into the grassy meadow, its tan coat providing perfect camouflage. A fine mist rose from the forest floor, and the ground glistened with dew. He watched through the binoculars as the deer flicked its white tail and craned an elegant neck to scan the forest, remaining motionless as the animal looked in his direction before returning its attention to feeding.

He crept forward a few paces and moved behind a tree.

The deer grazed forty yards away, its body turned in profile. He raised the rifle and centered the scope beneath the animal's shoulder, then he took a calming breath and tightened his finger on the trigger. The rifle's concussion kicked him backward a step and set his ears to ringing as he lowered the weapon and moved forward. The deer was a big male with mossy buds, and he could see the slug entered the animal's body precisely where he'd aimed. A dark rivulet of blood pulsed from the wound.

He ran his hand down its warm and twitching flank, staring at the animal's perfect form and appreciating the exquisite beauty of nature's creation. Guilt stabbed his heart as the life force faded from the animal's body. He whispered an apology, then unsheathed the skinning knife and hacked clumsily at the tough hide. He finally peeled it away and carved out a hefty slab of rich red meat.

He built a small fire, then cut a thick steak and dropped it in the pan. Soon it was sizzling, and the aroma aroused a carnivorous hunger to rise in his gut. He seized the meat and greedily ate until his stomach would accept no more.

He leaned back and inspected his bloody hands as he contemplated his marksmanship. He had fired the rifle twice on this journey, first at the jackrabbit and now the deer. Both times his aim was true. The weapon felt comfortable in his hands. Handling it was natural and automatic. Perhaps in his forgotten life, he'd been a soldier or outdoorsman.

He threw more hunks of venison in the pan, enjoying a sense of accomplishment. He was holding his own in the wilds. Bringing down game. Finding water. Moving nearer to home every day. No longer searching the sky and hoping for rescue. He remembered the row of corpses. Men who would never go home. He had rolled the dice and won. Setting out on his own had been the right decision.

He heard a rustling sound and leaped to his feet, scanning the woods for the grizzly. He resumed frying the venison, now thinking about the bear. Its behavior puzzled him. The animal was obviously stalking him, yet its actions didn't strike him as predatory. Appearing disinterested in him as prey, it had stared at him in what seemed a thoughtful, even intelligent manner. He was equally perplexed by his reaction. A dangerous forest animal was following him. His first impulse was to shoot it. He'd aimed the rifle at the bear's heart but couldn't bring himself to pull the trigger.

He sorted through his pack and found the baggie of coffee.

Filling the tin pot with creek water, he poured an ounce of grounds into the basket and set the pot on glowing embers. As it percolated, the familiar aroma brought forth a pleasant image. Sipping coffee on a shaded patio, a dog lazing at his feet. A garden with rows of rose bushes. A woman swaying to music. He strained to remember more as he ran his eyes across the forest's vast panorama. Majestic mountains framed endless miles of trees. The vista reminded him that he had far to travel. Every day he drew closer. He would eventually run across a road or town. Someone would have a phone.

He would use it to call Sarah.

Sarah?

He said the name aloud. A vault in his mind swung open, and a stream of memories tumbled out. The details of his life flooded into his head. His home. His wife. He realized the hovering angel in his dreams was Sarah. The whispered voice was hers. Other memories emerged as his mind unthawed. After a while, his mood turned somber as he remembered the last time he saw his wife. Now he knew the reason he'd boarded the aircraft. A heaviness settled around his shoulders as he poked at the fire's embers.

He kicked dirt on the fire and shouldered the pack. As he moved past the spot where he'd left the remains of the deer, he stopped short.

The carcass was gone.

The earth was dark with blood and entrails, but the animal had vanished. He'd built his cookfire not fifty yards from this spot. While he drank coffee and congratulated himself, something crept from the woods and carried off a hundred-pound deer carcass. Leaving no evidence. No bloody trail. No paw prints. No drag marks.

The grizzly hadn't committed the theft. It wasn't capable of such stealth. Something else had taken the carcass. What creature possessed the cunning and strength to pull off the heist? A wolf? Not likely. A pack would arrive noisily and tear into the carcass. A mountain lion came to mind, and but that didn't fit the scenario.

The woods felt different. Darker than an hour ago. Something had crept from the trees and snatched his kill. He had been oblivious to its presence. The animal could have as easily taken him. He shouldered his pack and moved out, now paying more attention.

Late in the day, he set up camp in a pretty meadow filled with bear grass and wildflowers. He started a fire and warmed up a hunk of deer meat. He watched the setting sun and the tensions of the day began to fade. He searched his backpack for the cigars, extracting a long stogie. He drew it under his nose and inhaled the fragrance of rain-soaked earth.

He put a match to it and took a long pull, rolling the cigar between his fingers. He poked the campfire with a stick and watched sparks jump into the night. His thoughts returned to the deer carcass, which now didn't seem so mysterious. He chuckled at his silliness and primitive fears. Ravenous monsters weren't creeping in from the shadows and stealing his food. There was a logical answer to the missing carcass. He'd bag another deer tomorrow, and this time keep a closer eye on it.

Darkness descended, and the sky became so densely packed with stars that they seemed crowded for space. Firelight cast shadows against the tall trees, and he watched them jerk like marionettes as the creek gurgled and a chorus of crickets serenaded him. He smoked the cigar to its ring before tossing the butt into the fire.

A comet flashed across the sky, leaving an arcing green contrail. He watched the object disappear behind a mountain and wondered if he'd glimpsed a glowing meteor or wayward spacecraft.

He fell asleep gazing at the stars and thinking of Sarah.

CHAPTER FOURTEEN

She awoke naked and shivering, immersed in a tub of ice water.

Raising a hand to her throbbing head, Sarah gazed in confusion around the room until realizing she was in her bathroom. She stood on shaky legs, waiting out a wave of dizziness before stepping from the tub and reaching for her bathrobe.

Music played from somewhere in the house and she staggered towards the sound, using walls to keep herself upright. She found Marcie in the bedroom closet, tunes blasting from her phone as she scrubbed vigorously at the carpet.

"What are you doing here?"

"Cleaning up your puke," Marcie said. She turned off the music, rising to embrace her friend.

Sarah stared at the stained carpet and released a moan of anguish. "Oh, my God," she cried, slumping to the floor.

Marcie dropped beside her and took Sarah in her arms. "Dumbass," she said softly. "What were you thinking?"

"I don't know," Sarah said miserably. "Everything seemed so hopeless, and I just gave up. Alcohol and stupidity don't mix, I guess." She sniffled on Marcie's shoulder and took deep shuddering breaths. "How did you know?"

"I've been worried about you since we got back from Seattle," Marcie said. "I knew it sucked all the hope out of you. Then you passed on my happy hour invites and didn't return my calls. Last night, I texted you a million times. I came to check on you and found you in the closet, passed out in a pool of vomit. By the way, I busted out your living room window. You don't remember any of this?"

"Very little."

"Just as well. I totally freaked out and got all hysterical. Slapped you around until you woke up. You told me you swallowed six pills, and I found them in the barf." Marcie rolled her eyes and shivered melodramatically.

"Yuck, by the way. Anyway, you begged me not to call 911, and you'd puked up the pills. I walked you around the house. You were pretty stinky and couldn't keep your eyes open, so I stuck you in the tub."

Marcie continued to chatter, and Sarah's memory unthawed as hazy memories of the night emerged. "I feel like an idiot," she said.

"You should feel that way," Marcie said. She locked eyes with her friend. "You should have called me."

"If I ever feel this way again, I'll call. But it won't happen again."

"You're sure."

"I'll never let myself get that low again, Marcie. I don't want to die. I want to be here when Evan comes home."

Marcie wouldn't leave until she'd fixed Sarah breakfast and extracted repeated promises that Sarah would call before doing anything stupid. Sarah slept most of the morning and awoke feeling even more ashamed. Last night she surrendered to weakness. She promised herself it would never happen again.

She felt the need to talk to somebody. Not Marcie. Her friend had just saved her life, and Sarah would forever love her for it. But right now, she didn't need a life coach. She needed someone who felt what she was feeling. Sarah scrolled through her phone and found the number of the perfect person.

Rose Flanagan's address was in the Encanto district of Phoenix. Sarah had listed several places in the historic area and knew most of the houses were built before World War II. Nearly all were restored and immaculately maintained, yards filled with fan palms and mature trees. Sarah drove slowly through the winding streets, following GPS directions and keeping track of house numbers.

She spotted Rose waving furiously from the front door of a cinnamon-colored pueblo-style house with massive logs jutting through the parapets. Even from the street, Sarah could see the large crucifix the woman wore around her neck. Rose greeted her with a hug and escorted Sarah into a Hacienda-style living room. Sarah paused to admire the Southwestern décor, arched doorways and hand-plastered walls. Wide exposed beams highlighted low ceilings, and Saltillo floors were covered with vibrant Mexican rugs. A huge picture of a matador poised to strike with a bloody sword hung above a flat-white beehive fireplace. Colorful couches were tastefully arranged around a long coffee table with wrought iron legs.

While Rose went to the kitchen to fetch wine, Sarah continued to look around the room. Depictions of Jesus adorned every wall. His head bathed in a crown of light. Jesus weeping with arms extended in benediction. A mural of the Last Supper, and of course one of Jesus wearing a crown of thorns. The inevitable crucifixion scene occupied center stage on one wall, and beside it a painting of Christ ascending into heaven.

Rectangular decorative cases holding tiny pieces of paper hung beside every doorway. Sarah stood before a large framed confirmation certificate. Bestowed to Rose Of Sharon Maisel and affirming her blessing at age eleven with the gift of the Holy Spirit.

Rose appeared with wine.

"You've discovered my dark secret." She smiled and handed Sarah a glass.

"Interesting name," Sarah said. They clinked and sipped.

"My mother was an Irish Jew," Rose said. "Raised in a little village outside Killarney. She converted to Catholicism as a teenager so she could marry my father. I guess it was quite the scandal in the Jewish community of her day. My mom had an eclectic religious identity, but she loved God with all her heart. She attended mass every Sunday and still worshiped at the synagogue. Dragged me with her every week. She found the perfect name for me in the Song of Solomon."

"You are a fascinating woman," Sarah said. She swept an arm around the room. "An Irish Catholic Jew who loves Mexican architecture."

"That's my husband's influence," Rose said. "My Gene was born in Tucson and loves the Southwest. Lived most of his life here. He's fluent in Spanish and I know he'd eat Mexican every day if I allowed it."

"What are those things?" Sarah had moved to the doorway and was pointing at one of the decorative cases.

"Mezuzah," Rose said. She smiled sheepishly. "A tradition carried over from my mother. The little piece of parchment inside the case is inscribed with Jewish prayers. You're supposed to have one in every doorway."

Sarah was now gazing at an ornately framed photo. Rose smiling into the camera, nearly hidden in the embrace of a man a foot taller. Thinning sandy hair. Handsome face and neatly trimmed mustache. Smiling in adoration at Rose.

"I know you miss him terribly."

Rose nodded, eyes glistening as she reached for the crucifix. "I don't know how to feel," she said. "If I grieve, I feel like I'm giving up. But too much hope makes me wonder if I'm in denial." She raised the crucifix to her lips and kissed it. "I can't stop thinking about what happened to my Gene. He's out there somewhere, maybe injured and hurting. All I can do is ask God to watch over him."

Sarah nodded towards the picture. "Tell me about him."

Rose gazed with adoring eyes at the photo. "The best husband in the world. We fell in love the moment we met. I married him at nineteen. He was my prince, and I was his princess. A fairy tale life, happily ever after, and all that stuff. He always says I'm one of his two great loves. The other is flying. He flew transport aircraft in the military and went straight to the commercial airlines after his discharge. Gene had a good career doing what he loved, and the past couple of years flew charters part-time for Air Pacific. When he isn't flying for work, he flies for fun. He keeps a little Cessna at the airport in Deer Valley. He's always tinkering with it and takes it up every chance he gets. Like I said, flying and me are all he cares about. I'm never sure which one he loves the most." She raised the cross to her lips and turned to Sarah.

"Tell me how you're holding up."

"Like you," she said. "I don't know whether to prepare for a homecoming or a burial. Most days I just go through the motions. One foot in front of the other. And my emotions are wild. One minute I feel numb and just want to sleep, and the next I'm running around like my hair's on fire."

"I know what you mean," Rose said.

"Some days are better than others. There are times I'm sure that today's the day he'll come walking through the door and this bad dream will end. Other times I'm convinced I'll never see him again."

They moved to the sofa and spent another hour drinking wine and sharing details of their lives. Rose brought out an album and they looked through snapshots of happier days. They speculated on what might have happened to the plane, where it went down, and how their husbands might have survived. Sarah asked Rose what she knew about the other passengers aboard the flight.

"A group of men," Rose said. "College buddies who get together every year for a big adventure. Gene's flown with them before. This time he was bringing them home from a hunting trip to Canada."

"I can't imagine why Evan was on that flight," Sarah said. "He wasn't due home until days later."

"He'll explain it when he gets home," Rose said. "I've included him in my prayers. Will you pray with me?"

Sarah closed her eyes and held Rose's hand as the woman prayed for the safe return of their husbands and the other passengers. She prayed for their souls and peace on earth. She asked God to enter Sarah's heart and give her strength. Prayer done, Rose said amen and wiped her eyes, then she poured more wine.

"I miss my Gene so badly," she said, "every minute of the day. But my heart is at peace. Whatever happens is God's will and I accept his wisdom. You believe, don't you?"

"I believe in Evan. He's the smartest man I know. And the most stubborn. Whatever he's going through, I know he'll figure out a way to overcome it."

"It's good that he's strong," Rose said, "but his life's in God's hands. We have to trust in his will."

Sarah smiled at her friend, saying nothing.

CHAPTER FIFTEEN

Something awoke him.

Kicking out of the sleeping bag, he sat up and scanned the clearing. A half-moon cast the night in an amber haze. The air felt heavy and charged with electricity. He raised his eyes, looking into the sky and wondering if a storm might be approaching. The fire had died down, and he tossed on a log that ignited and illuminated the clearing. He moved closer to the flames, welcoming their comfort.

There was a strangeness to the night.

Something was happening in the woods, some activity he couldn't see but his body recognized. A superstitious shiver ran up his spine. His heart hammered, his muscles bunched, and the hair on his neck prickled.

A flash of movement at the periphery of his vision. He caught a sinuous rippling in the darkness as shadows shifted and reformed. He hefted the rifle and racked a round, laying the weapon across his thighs.

Just outside the circle of firelight, a particular area

darker than the rest. He made out a shape. A vague silhouette. Barely perceptible movement. He narrowed his eyes, and it came into focus. An enormous humanlike form. Taller and broader than any person, staring at him with wide-set luminous eyes.

A high-pitched noise invaded the stillness, a million cicadas singing in unison. Something shifted in his consciousness. A wave of dizziness caused him to sway. Bubbles of carbonation streamed through his brain. He sank into unconsciousness. When awareness returned, the fire was glowing embers and the first streaks of dawn rising on the horizon.

The apparition was gone.

Tonight confirmed what he'd been suspecting. Some kind of creature was visiting him. Standing in the darkness. Watching him. He tried to think logically. What forest animal possessed a humanlike form and walked erect? Its gigantic silhouette suggested the animal weighed hundreds of pounds. It stood taller than an NBA ballplayer. Phosphorescent eyes. He immediately thought of the bear but dismissed the idea. A large grizzly might fit the silhouette. A bear was capable of standing on two legs. But nothing else made sense. This creature wasn't a bear. It was something else.

Bigfoot?

A laughable idea, but not at the moment.

Evan was familiar with the Bigfoot legend. He

had watched the shows. Read the articles. Stories had persisted for centuries, so prevalent they approached archetype. Bigfoot myths were common in every part of the world. North Americans called it Bigfoot. Native American tribes named the creature Sasquatch. Yeti had been sighted high in the Himalayas for nearly a century. Inuit legends spoke of the *Kushtuka*, a hairy creature with shining eyes that disappeared behind rainbows.

Bigfoot sightings were commonplace throughout the Northwest. Hunters reported seeing huge footprints in the region and hearing drum-like sounds attributed to the creatures pounding on tree trunks. Videos invariably depicted a large furry creature looking over its shoulder while running through the woods.

Credible scientists studying the phenomenon advocated new theories. Some speculated Bigfoot was an apelike species evolving in the wilds and avoiding human contact. The creature might represent a lesser evolved human relative. Some believed the creatures lived underground or in caves. There were the inevitable alien Bigfoot theories, and conspiracy theories abounded. Bigfoot hunters devoted their lives to finding them. Books were written and movies made about the creatures. Evan had consumed it all as entertainment, believing the stories interesting but ridiculous.

Now he wasn't so skeptical.

The skillet was still in the fire, keeping warm the last of his deer steak. He grabbed the meat and laid it at the edge of the woods. He returned to the fire and stoked it, then he rolled into the sleeping bag and watched the rising dawn as he thought about creatures of legend. Hours later, he rose and walked to the tree line.

The venison was gone.

In its place, a fresh green apple.

He spent six days traversing the primordial valley. The days were routine. The evenings surreal. The animal began making nightly visits, arriving during the darkest hours. He never heard a sound but knew when it arrived. Its form appeared beyond the firelight, translucent and shimmering. Then came the psychedelics. The atmosphere filling with white noise. Bubbles rising into his brain. Altering his reality. The creature's mind melding in some way with his before consciousness faded.

One night before sleeping, he left a granola bar at the edge of his campsite. The next morning, a deer haunch lay in its place. He squatted by the hindquarter and shook his head in wonder. He was bartering with a creature of the forest. Exchanging goods. A hunk of meat replaced with an apple. A haunch of venison swapped for a granola bar. The mystery of his disappearing deer carcass solved.

The night before he departed the primordial valley, the creature made a final visit. One he would forever remember. It began in the same manner. Heaviness in the air. White noise. The night's strangeness, as if time and space were warping. The silhouette materialized in the darkness. Pulsing and shimmering.

He heard a low rhythmic vocalization and realized it was speaking to him.

"What are you?" he said. His voice was raspy and hoarse.

He felt a light-headed rush, his mind frothy.

"Let me see you."

A hallucinogenic ribbon of light rolled through his mind, dreamy and swirling. Kaleidoscopic colors erupted around the animal's form. It vocalized again, expressing itself in a language he didn't understand.

"Come closer," he said. "Step into the light."

The apparition rustled. The space it occupied filled with a swirl of movement that reminded him of roiling water.

It stepped into the firelight.

"My God," he said.

CHAPTER SIXTEEN

Sarah stood in the threshold of his study, detecting the faint scent of a cigar. She detested the disgusting odor, but tonight the aroma brought an ache into her heart. This room was Evan's retreat, his quiet place where he would relax with a drink and cigar while working on his manuscript.

She wore one of his favorite dress shirts, with the sleeves rolled up. Silly and adolescent, but she didn't care. Sarah poured a shot of his favorite whiskey, wincing at the liquor's sharp bite. The room's emptiness caused aching loneliness to fill her heart.

She sat in his desk chair and closed her eyes, trying to feel his presence. Searching for him with her mind. Willing it to reach out and psychically connect with him. She remembered something he'd promised during their courtship. A silver strand would always connect their hearts, he told her. Infinite and invisible, this thread of love would forever connect them, regardless of the distance between them. She imagined this silver strand reaching across the universe and attaching itself to his heart.

The room was filled with his treasures. Mementos of vacations. A coffee mug from Montana. A tiny replica of the Eiffel Tower. Snapshots of ordinary moments, ones now bittersweet and precious. In every photograph, they stood with arms entwined while smiling into the camera.

Centered on the wall, a grainy black and white photograph.

Held in an ornate golden frame, the picture was a half-century-old and captured an image of five men. Two holding bulky acoustic guitars, one a fiddle. Another man with a guitar across his knees. The fifth grasping a washtub bass. Dressed identically. Overalls, work boots and grim expressions. This band of hillbilly musicians represented Evan's ancestry. The guitar players were uncles, the fiddler his grandfather. The man on the washtub his father. This photo was precious to Evan because it depicted his origins. He had traveled a long way from humble Appalachian roots, armed with little more than grit and ambition.

She'd come into the room to read his manuscript.

One of Evan's cherished dreams was to write a children's book. Lately he had been working on a story he called Jeremy's Journey. She felt a thickness in her chest as she opened the manuscript and read the tale of a lost boy traveling through a magical forest while trying to find his way home.

Tears began to flow, carrying with them the melancholy cool of a summer shower. She waited until the moment passed before returning her attention to the grainy picture. It never failed to give her hope, reminding her that Evan was descended from hardy country folk undeterred by deprivation or hardship.

If anyone could live through an airplane crash, it was Evan. If he were alone in the wilderness, it wouldn't intimidate him. He would find a way to survive. Nothing would stop him. He would crawl home if necessary. The idea was more than wishful thinking. The man at the airport, what was his name? Kelly? He'd told her that people survive airplane crashes. Some of them came home.

Sarah turned on the computer and began Googling survival stories.

Two men crashed a small plane in Alaska and survived for weeks on water and a can of salmon. A flight from Alberta to San Francisco crashed in the Canadian wilderness. In subfreezing temperatures, two people remained alive forty days by subsisting on melted snow and a tube of toothpaste. A pilot survived a crash in the Sierra Nevada mountains that killed a dozen people, suffering a broken leg but somehow crawling a hundred miles out of the mountains. A dozen crash survivors in Argentina lived through a winter in remote mountains.

Evan was coming home. She was convinced of it.

She shut down the computer and turned off the light in his study.

CHAPTER SEVENTEEN

He departed the primordial valley the next morning.

Following a winding game trail, he began the gradual ascent of a tall mountain. The path became increasingly steep, and by midmorning he was sweaty and tired. He crested the peak in early afternoon, relieved to see the terrain level out into a rocky plateau. He turned to take a last look into the ancient valley, suspecting that he was leaving Bigfoot's territory. After another hour's hike, he heard the rush of water. He followed the noise to a gushing stream and squatted to fill the canteens.

He enjoyed the water's musical sound, and the afternoon breeze cooled his forehead. He removed the green apple from his backpack and held it to the light. It was an object of unimaginable magnitude.

A gift bestowed by a forest creature.

Images of last night popped into his mind like exploding flashbulbs. The mysterious creature moving into the firelight, surrounded by a pulsating corona. Large and powerful, body coated in coarse fur, primate features. Not animal. Not human. A different species. The shimmering more intense as the creature moved towards him. Its face blurred and indistinct. Carbonation flaring through his mind as he faded into unconsciousness.

A nonexistent creature existed in these woods.

Neither human nor animal. A living entity like none he had ever encountered. Reaching out to him. Intelligent and curious. Causing him no harm. Speaking a language he did not understand. Capable of accessing his mind and making a psychic connection.

The conclusion was inescapable.

He had met Bigfoot.

The implications were mind-bending. Reality flipped upside down. Now any crazy belief was fair game. If Bigfoot existed, what about other creatures of legend? Leprechauns? Fairies? Sorcerers? Unicorns? Mermaids? Loch Ness monster? Why not aliens?

Why not God?

The question reverberated through his head. It presented a philosophical conundrum he couldn't begin to unravel. His religious upbringing was rooted in holy-roller Protestantism of Appalachia, beliefs he rejected as a teenager. During college, he fancied himself a Buddhist and dabbled with Catholicism. As he gained education and life experience, he drifted away from organized religion and became skeptical of God's existence.

Bigfoot and God. Putting them into the same thought seemed ridiculous.

But both represented the same paradox. Billions believed in God's existence. Vast numbers held a similar belief in Bigfoot. Not a shred of evidence had been found to prove either was real, and he'd spent his life convinced neither existed. Now he knew better. He had met Bigfoot, and that changed the game.

Today, anything was possible. Even God.

Weary with the effort of wrestling with the conundrum, he stretched out atop the sleeping bag. The gurgling stream pulled him into sleep, and he awoke no clearer in thought. He ate a chunk of venison before shouldering the backpack and preparing to return to the trail.

He stopped in his tracks and unslung his rifle.

A wolf sat thirty feet away.

The huge animal contemplated him with intelligent eyes, mouth open and panting as it exposed gleaming teeth. Ears upright and head tilted as it processed him. So motionless it might have been a statue, with only glittering eyes and lolling tongue revealing its life force. The wolf demonstrated no fear or aggression. It seemed to be studying him, perhaps curious at his presence in its domain.

He chambered a round and raised the rifle. The action caused the animal to react. It silently turned and padded into the forest. In an instant it was gone, disappearing into the trees. He held the weapon ready but saw no further sign of it. He put away the rifle and resumed his westward march.

He climbed a high bluff and gazed into the horizon. A succession of valleys ran like a string of pearls within an enormous rift carved by glaciers. These valleys wound through an extended mountain range and stretched as far as he could see. The nearest one was cut long and narrow, similar to Bigfoot's valley but lacking its primordial atmosphere. He spotted a considerable gorge cutting across its breadth, creasing the valley like a jagged scar. The rift terminated at the base of the high mountain to the north. A large lake covered much of the valley's midsection.

He ran binoculars along the gorge's vertical slopes and recognized the impossibility of crossing it. He decided to skirt the water along its southern shore and traverse the canyon at the far end. Once past the lake, he could bear north towards the mountains and find a way to cross the gorge.

He camped on the ridgeline, where he built a fire and cooked the last of the venison. Tomorrow would be a hunting day. He spotted V-lines of geese and wondered whether he might bring down one. He poured an ounce of bourbon into a tin cup and watched the sun drop behind the horizon.

Not for the first time, he wondered if he might be dreaming.

He'd never been this alone or so far from civilization. Maybe Bigfoot sightings, curious wolves, and stalking grizzlies were routine in the wilderness. He drew the cold night air into his lungs. Glittering constellations filled the heavens. He tasted the cup's cold metal and felt the whiskey's bite. He extended a hand to the crackling fire, jerking it away when flames heated his skin. He rubbed the stinging spot and decided he wasn't dreaming. He finished the whiskey and banked the fire before rolling into the sleeping bag.

Flickering strobes pulled him from sleep. A cosmic show was illuminating the night sky. He watched streaks of light flashing through the atmosphere like bolts of lightning. In the distance, a pulsing volcanic glow rose into the night. Crystal orbs of light danced within it, zipping about like fireflies. He rummaged for the binoculars and watched the radiance emanating from the jagged gorge.

This couldn't be the Northern Lights, the charged electrical particles from the sun that collided with the earth's atmosphere. The skies were clear, so he wasn't watching a lightning show. The spectacle continued an hour before the sky went dark, and the show ended as if someone hit a light switch. An atmospheric anomaly, he decided, random beams of heavenly light bouncing off earth's atmosphere.

He threw a log on the fire and watched the sky until he fell asleep.

CHAPTER EIGHTEEN

He set up camp beside the lake and dug out the fishing kit. After assembling the pole and attaching the reel, he turned over rocks until capturing a wriggling worm. He baited the hook and tossed in the line. A minute later, the line snapped straight, and he pulled in a good-sized trout. He cast again and reeled in another. He got the fire going and made a clumsy attempt to gut and clean the fish. He threw one in the pan and soon it was sizzling. He consumed every morsel and decided it was the most delicious meal he had ever tasted.

At dusk, he pulled out the binoculars. The light show began at midnight, as if on schedule. Streaks of light appeared without preamble and began racing across the sky, corkscrewing and soaring in wide loops. Some shot towards the heavens like rockets before plunging to earth and veering away an instant before colliding with the ground. A volcanic glow emanated from the gorge like red-hot charcoal, and he saw phosphorescent light dancing within it. The aerial performance occurred in near silence, except for a low humming that seemed to emanate from the chasm.

The streaks of light altered course and began flying above him. He gazed in rapture at their gyrations. It was evident the show was carried out purposefully, as the lights were far too precise and coordinated to be occurring randomly. The show continued for an hour, then the lights abruptly extinguished and it was over.

He slept soundly and awoke with a morning sun warming his face. He remained in the sleeping bag and stretched as he planned his day. He would enjoy trout for breakfast, then break camp and get going. He was nearing the gorge and wanted to reach it today. He was intent on identifying the source of the light show.

Something flashed through the periphery of his vision. A blur of gray.

The wolf stepped into the clearing. The animal stood stiff and erect, gleaming teeth bared and stiff tail extended. Its amber eyes opened wide, ears pointed forward, and a low growl rumbled from its chest. Its eyes shifted as the wolf looked past him, then he heard the chorus of growls and yips. Eight slavering wolves surrounded him, attention riveted on the alpha as they awaited the signal to attack. He returned his attention to the wolf. Their eyes met, and the rumbling went up a notch.

Then the animal was in motion, rushing towards him in powerful bounds. Still entangled in the bag, he could only duck inside and throw up an arm. The wolf slammed into him and latched massive jaws onto his forearm. He heard the crunching of bones and screamed in agony as the wolf tore at his arm. Only the sleeping bag kept the animal from tearing it off.

Another wolf slammed into him from behind and bit into his shoulder. Twisting and pulling in opposite directions, the two animals engaged in a brutal tug of war to tear apart his body. An excited howling rose from the pack.

He threw a shoulder into the alpha and tried to roll onto his side. He shoved again and felt the animal give way. The rifle and pistol lay on the ground beside the sleeping bag. He extended a hand and felt hard metal. He grabbed the gun, shoved the barrel against a wolf body, and pulled the trigger.

The crack of discharge was harsh and loud. The alpha fell away, and the one at his back released its grip. He scrambled from the bag and fired a round into a thrashing body. He turned and shot the other one. The yipping stopped as the pack melted into the woods.

The alpha still twitched and growled, and he put a slug in its head. He finished off the other wolf before collapsing onto the ground. His arm pulsed with pain. Blood seeped from a series of puncture wounds, and he felt a nasty bump rising along the radial bone. No doubt the arm was fractured. He shifted his body and felt a jolt of electricity run up his spine.

He rolled onto his stomach and tried to rise. A lightning bolt of pain forced him back to the ground. He crawled to a tree and pulled his body into a sitting position, laying the rifle across his thighs.

He remained awake through the night, wondering how soon he would die.

CHAPTER NINETEEN

Men in bars found Marcie irresistible. Tall and blonde, hair piled elegantly atop her head and wearing oversized glasses, her long legs and scandalously short skirts drew men like moths to a flame. Sarah had dressed appropriately for the place, so their chat was interspersed with a steady stream of suitors eager to buy drinks. Usually, she'd be flattered by the attention and might enjoy a harmless flirtation. Such things no longer mattered, and after a while the bar hounds moved on to more promising prospects.

"You don't look like a cast member of the walking dead anymore," Marcie said, leaning back to examine her friend. "Still taking the medication?"

Sarah nodded. "Religiously."

Marcie wagged a finger at her friend. "Don't go off them again." Sarah nodded again, and Marcie continued. "Now catch me up."

As usual, there was little to tell. Evan hadn't returned. Nobody was giving her any assurance it would ever happen. The mood swings were under better control, thanks to the medication. She was tending her roses, experimenting with some new ones. On occasion, she summoned the discipline to visit the yoga studio. An occasional pulse of energy rattled through her body or she felt the urge to do something stupid. She had learned how to shut things down before they spun out of control.

They were into their second glass of red wine when Marcie began cajoling her about returning to work. This wasn't a new topic. Sarah had adamantly rejected the idea each time Marcie brought it up.

"Okay," she said, stopping her friend in mid-chatter.

Marcie gave her a curious look. "Okay, what?"

"I'll come back Monday."

Marcie emitted a squeal and began prattling about deals in progress and new properties on the market. She launched into the latest office gossip. Sarah nodded and smiled but tuned out the monologue. Selling houses didn't interest her. She didn't care to know who was getting fired or divorced. Returning to work sounded awful, but anything was better than waiting for a call that never came. Marcie had charged on with her chattering, now asking if Sarah wanted to go out Saturday for drinks.

After hugging Marcie goodbye, Sarah sat in the car and experienced second thoughts. Going back to work still didn't feel right. She wondered if she was moving on too soon. Did it mean she was giving up on Evan?

She drove across town and parked in front of a high rise. Taking the elevator to an upper floor, she emerged an hour later with reddened eyes. She returned to the car, thinking of the man she had just left. Hoping he understood. Wondering if it mattered anymore. She started the engine and drove home.

The morning sun burned into his eyes and he startled awake. His back jerked into a wicked spasm as he tried to get to his feet. Rows of puncture wounds on his arm had turned ugly and purplish. He couldn't move his shoulder without agony. His body felt swollen and infected. His forehead burned with fever.

He slumped to the ground, panting with exhaustion. He wondered how long he could survive. His injuries were severe but survivable under ordinary circumstances. If the wolf attack occurred near civilization, a phone call would bring an ambulance and a gurney ride into the surgical suite.

In the wilderness, these wounds would kill him.

He wondered how the end would arrive. The best bets were infection or blood loss. They would kill him within days. Starvation was a distinct possibility. The scent of his blood was in the air and would surely bring predators. The wolf pack would probably return to finish their work. A cougar could wander by and investigate. The grizzly might decide to show up to finish him. If he managed to fight off wild animals, avoid infection, and stave off starvation, winter's cold would take him out.

His chances of survival were slim, but not impossible. He had the rifle to fight off predators and bring down game wandering into the meadow. The lake contained abundant water and fish. He possessed the means to build a fire. The weather was warm and winter months away, so freezing wasn't an immediate problem.

Tonight, he would build a signal fire. Commercial planes flew overhead, and he heard the occasional buzz of small aircraft. There was a chance one of these passing planes might spot his fire. The idea of making crutches came to mind, and he put the idea away for future consideration. He manipulated himself onto hands and knees, crawled into the trees, and gathered a small armful of wood. He set the sticks ablaze when dusk arrived.

The light show started precisely at midnight. The curtain in the sky rose, and the spectacle began. Flashing lights and arcing rockets filled the night, and the pulsing glow appeared above the gorge. The show was like nothing he had ever seen. He couldn't imagine what created it. He decided to give the signal fire another day or two, then he would crawl or drag himself to the canyon.

He pulled the sleeping bag over his head, but the pain wouldn't allow sleep. He gazed into the shaving mirror, seeing in its reflection a gaunt and filthy mountain man. He barely recognized the face staring back at him.

He drifted into fitful sleep awoke with his stomach spasming. He inched his way to the lake and threw in a line, snagging a crawfish and a small trout. He consumed the tiny creatures without bothering to cook them. He saw movement in the grass and spotted a long black snake. He grabbed the hatchet and crawled after it, severing the snake's spine. He cooked and ate every morsel of the flesh.

He cropped a branch into a splint, binding it to his shattered forearm with strips of shirt cloth. He trimmed low-hanging tree limbs and shaped them into crutches. He struggled to his feet and stuck the crutches under his armpits. He staggered halfway across the clearing before a spasm dropped him to the ground.

For the first time, he thought of surrender.

He closed his eyes, and his mind began to swirl as a kaleidoscope of sensations entered his consciousness. Murmurs. Bits and pieces of conversation. A whirring, metallic noise, and the distant sound of a radio. Arms embraced him, and Sarah's figure materialized above his head. Surrounded by a soft aura, her face wet with tears as she begged him to come home. His mind began rotating more rapidly as if circling a drain, then he dropped into darkness.

He awoke shivering. The night sky was bright with streams of light that arced high before plunging towards the earth. There and gone in an instant, each flash of illumination was followed by another close behind. He watched the streaks of brilliance flare and die.

His light would soon blink out. He lay on the cold ground and pondered the insignificance of his life. It had passed as quickly as the tracers in the sky. He harbored no grand illusions about his time on earth. It amounted to a grain of sand in the desert. He had accomplished nothing remarkable, left behind no progeny, made no lasting mark. His legacy would consist of little more than a troubled marriage and an incomplete career. Sarah would shed her tears. His obituary might merit sympathetic thoughts. The world would continue to revolve as if he had never existed. He drifted back into sleep, wondering if he would die tomorrow.

A splashing noise from the lake awoke him.

He rose onto an elbow and looked across the meadow. A grizzly prowled the lake's far side. He recognized the patch of white on its rump and had no doubt this was his bear. He smiled as he watched it romp back and forth along the water's edge. The bear began slapping huge paws onto the surface. It plunged its head into the water and emerged with a wriggling trout. The grizzly carried the catch to a sunny meadow and began tearing at it.

Done with its meal, the bear rolled onto its back, extending enormous paws into the air as it wriggled on the grassy field. It rose onto haunches and looked across the lake, flaring wide nostrils and testing the air. The bear caught his scent and looked in his direction before lumbering into the forest. It stopped at the tree line and swiveled its big head, as if waiting for him to follow. It rumbled into the trees and was gone.

He stuck the rough-hewn crutches under his arms, waiting until the dizziness passed before hobbling to the lake. He found a worm beneath a flat rock. After a dozen casts, he reeled in a small trout. He bit into the struggling fish, tearing away its meager flesh before tossing away the tiny skeleton.

He dumped the backpack's contents, selecting things he would need for the final leg of his journey. The rifle and binoculars. Canteens of water and bourbon. He stuck a cigar and lighter in his shirt pocket. Everything else he left scattered on the ground.

He hefted the rifle, put the crutches in place, and began moving towards the jagged ravine. He figured to make it by late tomorrow. He would look into it and discover the source of the cosmic light show.

Then he would throw himself into the gorge.

CHAPTER TWENTY

Sarah located their seats in the first-class section. Marcie slid in next to her, flushed and giggling with excitement. They settled into wide leather seats, sipping Mai Tai's and watching the stream of coach passengers file past. Marcie kept poking her ribs and laughing while raising her drink for toasts. They wore floral muumuus and sandals, and each had a purple orchid in her hair.

They were going to Hawaii.

Sarah had returned to work and dove headfirst into the hectic world of residential real estate. Marcie insisted they team up to form a powerhouse sales force, and on Sarah's first afternoon back they landed a two-million-dollar listing on a three-acre hillside palace in Paradise Valley. Three days later, a full price cash offer dropped in their laps. The deal was quickly consummated, escrow and closing a breeze, and they split a hundred and forty thousand-dollar commission.

Marcie insisted they celebrate by going to Hawaii. Sarah wasn't interested in a vacation, a preference that evidently failed to register on Marcie. Once in her head, she wouldn't let go of the idea. Marcie endlessly beat the drum, placing brochures on Sarah's desk, wearing a muumuu to work, and piping Hawaiian music through the office. She unleashed a torrent of texts, sending Sarah a succession of photos depicting the wonders of Hawaii. Marcie kept telling her a vacation would do her good. Energized by the seventy-thousand-dollar commission, Sarah began seeing the trip differently. Setting aside her problems a few days wouldn't hurt anything, and jetting off to Hawaii with Marcie might be fun.

It was the least she could do. Marcie was her rock and her best friend. She knew Sarah's worst secrets and continued to love her. She cared enough to break into Sarah's home and stop her from an act of terminal stupidity, and then she cleaned up the puke. Marcie cajoled her into resuming work and essentially gifted Sarah with a seventy-thousand-dollar commission. If her friend wanted Hawaii, then Sarah would go with her.

Now, sitting in a luxury seat that would lay flat and holding a tropical drink with a pineapple wedge and umbrella, Hawaii seemed like a grand idea. The flight attendant brought another round of tropical drinks while Marcie chattered non-stop about the things they must do in Maui. Massages on the beach. Snorkeling. Sailing a catamaran and learning to surf. They would meet interesting people, go to clubs, and dance all night. The trip would be the adventure of a lifetime.

She reclined her seat until it was horizontal and dozed off while Marcie continued her monologue about their island adventure. They checked into a large suite at a five-star hotel located on the beach. They stood on the lanai drinking more Mai Tai's while gazing at the busy beach scene. Throngs of vacationers clad in colorful bathing suits walked or skated in every direction. The pool was crowded. Beyond it lay the gorgeous blue of the Pacific and another gaggle of vacationers splashing at the shore. Marcie spotted the thatched roof of a Tiki bar adjacent to the pool.

"Let's go," she said.

They spent six days enjoying the aloha lifestyle. They tanned on the beach. Watched the sun rise from atop a volcano, then biked down the mountain with Marcie screaming all the way. They drove the road to Hana in a convertible. Evenings they visited fine restaurants and danced in noisy clubs. Sarah became caught up in the exotic locale and Marcie's boundless energy. Island amnesia struck her, and she began having a ball.

As always with Marcie, men flocked in their direction. Two showed particular interest. Adam and Brian. Both young, handsome and charming. As the night progressed, there was a pairing off. Marcie with Adam. Sarah with Brian. Sarah found herself gyrating with him on the dance floor. At evening's end, they agreed to meet the following night for more fun. The men took them to dinner at an expensive restaurant on the water. They walked barefoot on the beach before returning to the bar for drinks.

Marcie was somewhere with Adam, and Sarah had no doubt the young man would get lucky tonight. Sarah was tucked into a darkened booth with Brian, talking and laughing over the noise of the bar. Brian lived in San Francisco and made his money doing something in the stock market. Funny and good-looking, he made no effort to hide his interest, and Sarah felt a growing attraction to him. Late in the evening, Brian smiled and leaned towards her. She felt a charge of anticipation and started to move towards him, then Evan's image filled her head and jolted her into reality. She moved away and stood up.

"I'm sorry," she said, and ran for the door.

She walked in darkness along the foaming surf. What the hell was she doing? She'd been about to make out with a man in a bar. Who knew what else she might have done? The last thing she needed was a fling, and she couldn't believe her foolishness in running off to Hawaii with Marcie. She hadn't taken her medication all week, and the magic of the islands had her in its spell. She was a married woman, filled with guilt and still desperately hoping for her husband's return. She had barely pulled out of an emotional abyss so deep she'd swallowed a handful of pills. Battling a mental illness she barely kept chemically caged, she was determined to never again fall apart or commit acts of self-destructive stupidity. It was time to go home.

Someone approached from behind.

"I'm sorry," Brian said. She saw the softness in his face, and pent-up emotions overflowed. She hated blubbering in front of him but was unable to stop the tears. He held her tightly as she sobbed into his chest.

"I'm such a crybaby," she said. "I know it's not what you had in mind for this evening."

He stroked her hair and murmured into her ear, and then he released her with a gentle smile. "If you want to tell me about it, I'm ready to listen."

She exhaled and searched his eyes for sincerity. "It's not a happy story. You sure you want to hear it."

"I do," he said.

She took his hand and they walked along the beach, the surf foaming that their feet. She told him everything as they strolled towards the sea wall a mile down the coast. The early years and her happy marriage to Evan. The beginning of her illness and the foolish affair. The disappearance of Evan's plane and the agonizing wait for his return. The guilt and depression she battled every day. The impossible dilemma of waiting for Evan while trying to move on with her life. Hawaii was supposed to provide a break from it, yet she had managed to create another mess.

Brian listened silently, then he pulled her to him and told her he understood and not to worry about him. He assured her that he wouldn't ask her to do anything she didn't feel right about doing and offered to walk her to the hotel.

It was the perfect thing to say. She put her arms around his neck and hugged him.

CHAPTER TWENTY-ONE

He threw down the crutches and slumped to the ground, his back arcing with spasms. Body throbbing. Knees and hands a bloody mess. Gathering rain clouds finally burst open, saturating his body. He began gasping for breath as he lay shivering on the cold earth.

A feeling of warmth gradually infused his body, as if someone threw a comforter over him. His shivering stopped and the pain faded, leaving him with a pleasant feeling of numbness. He rolled onto his back and stared into the night sky.

Wondering what would happen next.

Would angels descend from billowing clouds accompanied by sounds of celestial harps, escorting him to a kingdom in the sky? Were pearly gates preparing to swing open, and beyond them parents and relatives waiting to greet him? Would departed pets run joyously to him? Would he stand before God and account for his sins? Or would a vessel ferry him across the Styx and through the fiery gates of Hell? Would he return to the raft on a meandering river and float to the city in the clouds? Or would he simply blink out and spend eternity in darkness? His dying body convinced him that he would soon know the answer.

The rainy night didn't deter the light show. Tracers of light appeared and slashed across the sky. Some zoomed low, running inches above the tree line. Others flashed over his head, pausing to hover before streaking away. A pulsating throb reverberated through the gorge, setting his body to vibrating.

He watched the show until it ran its cycle and ended.

He awoke with morning's light, again cold and shivering. He rolled over and resumed crawling. He spent the day scrabbling across hard ground, stopping more frequently to wait out spasms of pain. He dragged himself atop a small hill and spotted the gorge a hundred yards distant. Exhausted, he fell asleep.

When he awoke, the glow was pulsing from the gorge, flashing like a railroad warning signal. He felt the heat as its energy shimmered into the night. A dome of iridescent light enclosed the gorge, extending miles into the sky. Crystal orbs danced inside the light. He now saw they were gigantic ball-shaped structures of shiny metal, their exteriors brilliant and multi-faceted as if reflecting the light from a million diamonds. Metallic tentacles snaked from them, extending multi-hinged arms into the gorge. Darting lights flashed overhead like comets.

He turned from the lights and made final preparations.

He lit the stogie. Uncapped the canteen with a steady hand. He raised it to the skies and savored a final shot of bourbon. He smoked the cigar to the ring and drained the canteen, thinking of Sarah.

He recalled his favorite image of her. Standing beside him on their wedding day, glorious in her gown, her face radiant with love. He held her face in his mind and whispered a final goodbye.

He realized the dome encasing the gorge was actually a shimmering curtain of light. He stepped inside the translucent barrier. His body began vibrating like a tuning fork. He felt a mild electrical charge. He stepped closer to the canyon floor and felt the warmth emanating from it. The dancing lights were close enough to touch. The gigantic bubbles with dangling metallic arms floated above his head. Low throbbing hammered his eardrums as the lights pulsed brighter, dancing like demented fireflies.

He moved forward and peered into the gorge.

"My God," he said.

A spacecraft hovered above the floor of the ravine. Enormous and pulsing, the craft was the size of a city block. Metallic orbs ferried back and forth, extending shiny tentacles to the ground, glistening claws extracting massive handfuls of soil before returning to the mother ship. Glowing lights emanated from a line of portholes, and he saw elongated shadows scurrying past them. Cavernous hatches spaced around the ship's body. Saucer-shaped craft darted in and out like busy bees, trailing contrails of multicolored light.

Nothing about the scene surprised him. The appearance of a spaceship made as much sense as Bigfoot or a friendly grizzly bear. Why not a spaceship carrying visitors from the stars? Was it a dream? LSD flashback? It no longer mattered.

A sense of peace entered his body as he pulled himself to his feet and staggered to the edge of the ravine. He uttered a final goodbye to Sarah, closed his eyes, and extended his arms. Gravity pulled his body forward.

He plunged into the gorge.

———◆———

He awoke in a sun-dappled field, raising a hand to shield his eyes from the morning light. The day was bright and sunny, and tall conifers framed the cobalt sky. Earth's colors were unnaturally vivid. The pleasant buzzing of insects rose above the silence, and a cooling breeze wafted across his forehead.

He gazed down at his perfect body.

He raised the arm savaged days earlier by wolves. Gone were jagged puncture marks, the engorged knot at the spot of the fracture, and the ugly yellow-purple discoloration. He made a fist and rotated his wrist, flexing his arm into a muscle. He stood and rotated his back, arching it and spreading his arms wide. He bent to touch his toes. Lithe and athletic, his body had regained the vitality of a teenager.

He tried to comprehend it. Last night he jumped into the gorge. This morning he was alive and healthy. His wounds miraculously healed. He walked to the edge, covering the ground with long and graceful strides. Scrubby pine covered the valley floor, and a stream meandered down its length. A herd of elk grazed on the creek's far side, and birds flitted among the trees. A hawk glided effortlessly above the canyon.

No spacecraft. No alien miners.

Memories flickered in his mind. The shimmering curtain. The mother ship. Spacecraft streaking through the air. Metallic bubbles floating like translucent jellyfish, tentacles plunging claws into the earth, rising and carrying minerals to the ship. The rush of wind on his face as he plunged towards his death. His fatal fall stopped in midair. Rising through a bright blue beam towards a hovering craft.

Interplanetary travelers had saved his life.

There was no other explanation. He had encountered an expedition of intergalactic miners, alien visitors who stopped his suicidal plunge and lifted him into their ship. They healed his wounds and returned him to perfect health.

He tried to imagine another explanation for experience in the gorge. Something logical or earthly. Nothing else fit the facts. He made his way back to the lake, where he gathered his belongings.

He studied the sun's position, hefted the backpack, and began hiking along the eastern edge of the gorge. Aiming for a line of snow-covered mountains. He moved effortlessly through the woods, his long stride eating up miles. Feeling stronger and more limber than any time in his life, energy surged through his body as a sense of well-being infused him. There was a reason he was still alive. He couldn't wait to discover it.

CHAPTER TWENTY-TWO

He made steady westward progress, enjoying his new body and a sense of well-being. Each day dawned sunny and warm, and the forest teemed with growth. Trees sang with the melodic chirping of birds. Gushing streams were abundant with trout. One afternoon he spied movement on a faraway sloping hill. Raising binoculars, he spotted a rumbling herd of elk. He fell in behind them, following the herd as it moved up the slopes towards cooler elevation. He crept close and raised the rifle, bringing down a large bull. That evening he sat by a warm fire and savored the delicious meat.

The forest began to reveal more of its bounty. He picked tart berries from a thatch of bushes. Honeybees swarming around a rotted apple alerted him to the tree. Harvesting all he could cram into his backpack, he crunched into one as he trekked onward. He took an afternoon break, laying beneath a shady tree in a meadow filled with dandelions.

He plucked one and twirled it between his fingers.

The flower brought into his mind a flood of memories. A slanting row of shanty houses flung along a one-lane dirt road. Growing up in a three-room shack without electricity or plumbing. Pumping water from a village pump and hauling it to the house in a shiny bucket. Doing his business in a rickety outhouse stocked with a Sears catalog. Sleeping beside three brothers beneath quilted covers in a tiny back bedroom. Swinging on a knotted rope. Fighting imaginary battles with stick rifles.

He remembered a heavy iron stove in the middle of the living room, its light illuminating his mother's face as she poked at glowing coals. The sound of rifle fire echoing through the forest, and his father slinging squirrel or rabbit onto a wooden table.

The memory of his father brought a smile to his face. A lean man with a jaunty walk who burst through the door every night, miner's hat askew and face black from coal dust. A plug of Red Man in his cheek and spittle on his chin. Singing an off-key limerick and reaching into his pocket for the pint of bathtub gin. Smiling and pointing the bottle at him before raising it to his lips.

A long-ago hunting trip came to mind.

He and brother Lucas accompanied his father and a pack of uncles on a game hunt, a grand adventure for a boy of ten. They'd hunted deer in valleys similar to those he was now traversing. He remembered firing a .22 rifle at squirrels while the men hunted larger game. Wary of copperheads and mine shafts as he scoured the woods for greens for the dinner pot. Chicory and daylily. Scallions and chanterelles. Dandelions. The joyous feeling of uncles slapping his back when he divulged the location of a treasure trove of precious ginseng.

The men stalked game all day and built campfires at night. Jugs of homebrew passed around while uncles told bawdy jokes and dispensed mountain wisdom. Fiddles and banjoes and hillbilly music filling the night.

As the fire died down, the men told stories, most designed to scare young boys. His favorite was the yarn his father spun about a mysterious hunting trip to Horsemill Holler. He hadn't heard the story since childhood, but he remembered the chill he felt when his father leaned forward and spoke in a low and conspiratorial voice.

Now some years back, me and your uncles went ahuntin' up Horsemill Holler. Most a' the men wouldn't go up there, but times was lean and game scarce so we decided to go. Soon's we got in that holler, a spooky feelin' came over us. Place jest didn't feel right. It was dead quiet. Not even the birds was a'chirpin. No frogs croakin'. Nary a sign of life. The dogs couldn't scare up anything. Not even a squirrel. Then all of a sudden them dogs flushed somethin' and went tearing off after it, bayin' like they was chasin' Satan hisself. We figured they were running down a ba'ar or maybe they'd a' treed a panther.

We chased 'm two or three miles up that holler and finally caught up. Them dogs weren't after a ba'ar and wasn't standin' below no tree. They was circled around a big hole in the ground, jumpy and nervous, an' them dogs had gone quiet. We come up on that hole and looked down in it, but it was black as night. I shined a light in there and didn't see the bottom. I didn't see no critters, neither.

We stood around a while, tryin' to figure out what to do, when all of a sudden the dogs got spooked and run off. They ran all the way out of that place and we didn't see 'em again 'til we got back home. We had nothin' for the dinner pot and I wanted to root out that critter, so we got out our shovels and commenced to diggin'.

Jest then a growlin' noise came up out a' that hole. A spooky, echoin' sound like I never heard before or since. Not animal or human. Some other kinda critter was dug in there. We was curious to see it, so we kept on a' diggin'. All of a sudden another sound come up from that hole, a deep and evil-soundin' voice that spoke to us. "If you'll leave me alone, I'll leave you alone," that thing said to us. I felt somethin' run up my spine, like I never felt before, and I took to shiverin' like I had the fever.

I jumped back from that hole and looked at the boys. They looked like they'd a'heard the Devil hisself. "Let's get the hell out of here," I said, and we hightailed it out of Horsemill Holler and ain't never gone back.

Now you boys don't go playin' up in that place. There's something livin' in a hole up there, and you don't want to meet it.

The story ended the same. An uncle would sneak up and yank the boys backward, resulting in shrieks and laughter. The tale was scary enough that he and Lucas were careful to never venture into Horsemill Holler. Now he smiled at the thought of his father's cleverness. As a teenager, he learned his father and uncles kept a still in that holler. The story was a clever way to keep curious boys from discovering it.

He shouldered the backpack and bent to grab a handful of dandelions. That evening he tossed them into the skillet with the meat. They gave the venison a nutty and mildly bitter taste, and they added variety to his protein diet.

He rose at daybreak, located his landmark on the horizon, and marched towards it. The day passed uneventfully, and he set up camp by a small stream. He ran a finger across the well-worn route map, wanting to identify the mountain range to the north. If he could pinpoint it, he might fix his location and calculate the remaining distance home. His concentration was broken by a sound drifting in on the wind. A low-pitched buzzing, as if a swarm of angry hornets was headed in his direction.

He squinted into the sun and spotted the aircraft.

It was angling towards the ground and heading for him. He jumped to his feet, screaming and waving his arms. He grabbed the rifle and fired off a round as the plane flew past, engine roaring as it dropped towards the treetops. Seeing no waggle or sign of recognition, he scrambled up a conifer and spotted the aircraft through the binoculars. Its flaps were lowered as the plane dropped through the trees towards a dirt runway. A wide river ran next to the airstrip. No more than five miles away. He raised a fist and let out a yell of triumph.

His transportation home had arrived.

CHAPTER TWENTY-THREE

At first light, he set off to locate the landing strip. His face creased into a smile as he imagined the coming day. It would be the best one of his life. An easy walk through the woods. Home by tomorrow and a joyous resumption of his life. The conclusion of a life-changing journey. The beginning of a new one.

Talk about a miracle ending.

His journey began with an airplane ride. It would end with one. He imagined how the world might react to his miraculous reappearance. Shock and amazement, he figured. He tried to envision the reunion with Sarah. Would she be happy to see him? Disappointed? He felt excited in anticipation of seeing her. Her infidelity now seemed trivial and he was confident they would work things out.

He chuckled at the thought of trying to explain his survival story to the world. The crazy experiences. Impossible encounters. The close calls with death. He wondered if anyone would believe any of it.

He stopped to rest atop a gnarled log, taking a long

drink from the canteen. He allowed himself a moment of pride. Against all the odds, he had lived through an air crash that killed sixteen men. Walked away from possible rescue and embarked on a solitary trek through hundreds of miles of wilderness. Trusted in his skills and determination. Lived off the land. It was the stuff of an adventure movie.

Few would appreciate the obstacles he'd overcome. Not many understood the mixture of terror and elation one experienced when standing at the precipice of death. Thrill-seekers might know the feeling. He recalled an adventurer who floated solo around the world in a hot air balloon. A teenager sailed alone across the Pacific. A daredevil jumped from an airplane without a parachute, landing in a net. Another man parachuted from the edge of space.

A man spent a year camping among grizzlies in remote Alaska. The bears eventually attacked and devoured the adventurer, and the world vilified him as a fool. Evan could appreciate the man's motivations. Living among earth's most dangerous beasts, a heartbeat from death, must have provided an intoxicating rush. For such people, an exploit wasn't worthwhile if life wasn't at risk. He figured the difference between adventure and disaster was whether you survived the experience.

A buzzing startled him from his reverie.

The plane passed overhead, sharply banking as it rose into the sky. He jumped to his feet and waved, shouting himself hoarse as the aircraft disappeared into the horizon. He dropped to his knees and pounded the ground. He'd been an hour from rescue. Then he remembered the airstrip. Someone built it for a reason. The aircraft probably ferried in hunters or fishermen. There would be an encampment. The plane would return.

Hope renewed, he began walking towards the airstrip. As he drew closer, a dense, rhythmic thumping came reverberating through the trees. He cocked his head to listen, then he continued towards it. As he drew closer, he heard music blasting through speakers, cranked up to maximum volume.

The rasp of a demonic voice rose above the din, grunting and belching a stream of indecipherable lyrics. He recognized metallic punk music of the kind he despised, although at the moment it was the most glorious noise on earth. Someone was at the camp, and their musical taste didn't matter.

Sharp cracks rang out. He dove for cover, figuring hunters were firing at game or targets. More shots erupted, then the music abruptly shut off. He waited until the shooting stopped before stepping from concealment and moving to the edge of the clearing. Lifting the binoculars, he spotted a campsite set up in a small clearing. Tents pitched near a crude fire pit. Nearby, the rutted tracks of the airstrip running the length of a grassy meadow.

A man and woman stood in front of a tent. The man was barefoot and wearing only blue jeans, his naked upper body thick and chiseled like a bodybuilder. Arms obscenely swollen and steroidal. Long unwashed hair pulled into a ponytail. A fat gold chain around his neck. Face flushed, and mouth pulled into a sneer, he was holding a pistol to the woman's head and a metal rod in his other hand.

The man fired the pistol into the air and bellowed, causing the woman to flinch, then he jabbed her with the rod. She convulsed and fell to the ground, body jerking and trembling. The brute towered over her, still yelling in an angry voice. Evan trained the binoculars on the man's face. He was about thirty and had a hard look about him. His face contorted as he continued to shout at the woman.

The woman was young, maybe thirty. Filthy, wearing only panties and a bra, her face smeared with makeup. A shackle fastened to her ankle, a long chain extending to a metal stake. She raised her hands towards the man, obviously begging him to stop. Evan ran the glasses down her body and saw ugly welts on her arms and legs. The man was using a cattle prod. The brute threw the prod to the ground and grabbed a fistful of hair, dragging the sobbing woman inside the tent.

Evan's face flushed and he struggled for breath as a fulminating rage seized him. He felt a savage desire to batter the brute to the ground. He unslung the rifle and crept through the woods, reaching the opposite side of the clearing. He stepped from the shadows and approached the tent from the backside, creeping close enough to hear the sounds of slapping bodies, the woman's painful moaning, and the man's thrusting grunts.

He crept past the tent and positioned himself beside the entrance flap. He threw the rifle over his shoulder and reached for the hatchet. Its head was cast iron, sharp on one end and blunt on the other. He waited as the pathetic cries and animalistic grunts grew louder. Finally, the man emitted a series of hoarse groans, followed by the rustling of clothing.

A tattooed hand pushed aside the tent flap and the man stepped outside, breathing heavily, face flushed from his exertions. He yawned and stretched his muscled body, and then he reached for a cigarette jammed behind his ear. He pulled a lighter from his jeans and stuck the cigarette between his lips.

Evan stepped forward and raised the hatchet, slamming the blunt end into the side of the man's head. He felt a crunch as the skull gave way, and a spray of blood misted his face. The man dropped moaning to the ground. Evan swung twice more, shattering the man's elbow and knee, then he knelt and rifled the brute's jean pockets for a key.

He pulled open the tent flap and stepped inside.

The woman lay curled into a corner, staring at him with frightened eyes.

"I'm here to help," he said softly. He held up the key and nodded towards the shackle on her ankle.

He saw the emotions ripple through her face. Confusion. Terror. Then dawning comprehension and relief as she extended a trembling leg. He removed the lock and pulled off the steel cuff. He stepped back and took a close look at her.

Her humanity was concealed beneath a mask of horror. Her body was covered in filth, and her face grotesque with streaked makeup. A smear of red lipstick encircled her mouth, and her eyes were lined with thick mascara. The makeup caused her to look cartoonish, and he knew the brute had applied it. She rose on unsteady legs, dropping her eyes as she brushed past him and stepped through the tent flap.

He watched as she crossed the meadow and waded into the river, where she immersed her body in the icy water. She scrubbed earnestly at her face and spent a long time on the area between her legs. Her sobbing floated above the river's noise. He returned to the tent and spotted a pile of clothing. A lady-size sweatshirt and yoga pants. A folded towel. He laid it all on a flat rock near the water before returning to the camp.

She stepped out of the river and dried herself, slipped on the clothing, and walked towards him. River water had washed away most of the makeup, and now he could see that she was a beautiful young woman. Her body was tall and curvaceous, her hair dense and black, and her skin a pale olive. Her fragile face was hidden beneath a mass of bruises and a purple shiner that rose beneath an eye. Fresh blood trickled from her ear. Ugly burns and welts covered her arms and legs.

She brushed past him, body trembling as she moved towards the man on the ground. She stood over him, her breath rasping as she picked up the cattle prod and jabbed his stomach. The man spasmed as high voltage shot through his body. She muttered something and gave him another jolt. She was preparing to juice him again when Evan gently pulled her away and took the prod from her hand.

"You have every right," he said. "He deserves worse. But we need to get you away from this place."

She spat on the man before going into the tent and returning with the shackle. She clamped it onto his ankle and gave him a final kick in the ribs. For the first time, she raised her eyes to meet his and rendered the smallest nod of recognition.

"Anyone else here?" He asked.

She shook her head.

"Who's in the airplane?"

"His brother," she said. "Worse than him. He's coming back in the morning."

Evan ran his eyes around the camp. "What's this about?"

"They drugged me," she said. "Brought me here and had their fun. They were going to kill me tomorrow."

Her voice was flat and dispassionate, and her body continued to tremble and jerk. He could only imagine what she'd endured in this place.

"Who are you?" she said.

"I survived a plane crash a few weeks ago and I'm headed home. You can join me, if you want."

She said nothing.

"What's your name?"

"Andrea," she said.

He jerked his head towards the sky. "If the other one's coming back, we better get out of here."

He walked through the camp, filling a duffel with anything useful. Canned meat. Cold cuts and cheese in a cooler. A few bottles of water and a jug of premium whiskey. A bundle of Cuban cigars. He walked past a camp table covered with baggies. Pills. Weed. A white powder.

A holster and belt hung on a camp chair. He took them and retrieved the pistol from the tent. Andrea was at the camp table, staring at the assortment of drugs. She picked up a double handful and stuffed them into her pocket. He handed her the duffel and gun belt.

He returned to kneel beside the unconscious man. The hatchet had punched a nasty hole in his skull, and blood oozed from an ugly laceration. Welts were rising on his stomach. A bone protruded from his elbow, and the knee was bloody and misshapen. Evan gazed at the man's brutal face and heard his groans of pain. He turned to look at the devastated woman, then he stood and walked away.

Andrea waited at the edge of the clearing, duffel slung across her back and pistol strapped to her waist. He walked past her and into the woods.

She fell in behind him.

CHAPTER TWENTY-FOUR

Sarah walked out of the courtroom and accepted a hug from her attorney. Brad Nixon was a golfing buddy of Evan's. Following the aircraft's disappearance, Nixon called expressing condolences and offering his legal services. She couldn't imagine needing a lawyer, but time passed and circumstances changed. She was facing financial ruin. Running out of money. Mortgage and car payments were eating up her income. Bills were piling up, checking and savings accounts depleted, and real estate sales had slowed. She was slowly sinking further underwater.

Something had to be done, and she hoped the attorney might throw her a lifeline. Nixon was a tall and angular man who spoke fondly of Evan. They spent an hour talking legalities before he assured Sarah that he could help her. He needed only to file a petition for a finding of death, along with a statement of circumstances. He explained that Arizona law required a five-year waiting period unless extraordinary circumstances existed.

Nixon was confident the airplane crash and Evan's situation met the criteria. In such cases, courts were almost certain to waive the five-year period. The lawyer wrote and filed the motion, and scheduled the hearing. He refused to accept a fee, insisting it was the least he could do for a friend.

This morning Sarah spent five minutes in front of a Superior Court judge, who briskly scanned the packet of legal documents. Nixon had been correct in his prediction. The judge responded kindly to her petition and granted the motion. He advised her to return to court in thirty days. If there were no developments, he would direct the county medical examiner to issue a certificate of death. Evan would become deceased in the eyes of the state.

The midday temperature was approaching 115 degrees as she left the courthouse. Working through lunchtime Phoenix traffic, she turned up the air conditioner and aimed its vents at her face. Beads of sweat formed on her forehead as she made her away across town. The next stop was the insurance agent.

She spent an hour reviewing her policy, filling out forms, and providing affidavits. The agent advised her that he saw no problem with the claim as long as she could provide the death certificate. Sarah assured him she would have it in a month. Shimmering waves of heat radiated from the blacktop lot as she returned to the car. Sarah sat motionlessly and stared at the documents in her hands.

Thirty days from today, Evan would be legally dead.

She pounded the steering wheel as she cried, unable to shake the feeling that she was betraying him. This paperwork represented surrender, an abandonment of belief that he would return.

How long do I wait?

She'd asked herself the question a thousand times. Spent countless hours debating it with Marcie. When do you resume living? How long before you can move on? A year? Five years? A decade? Never? Marcie was blunt with her opinion on the matter. It was time to stop grieving and get back to living.

Her financial predicament left her with no choice but to start planning a life without Evan. Retaining the attorney had been a start. She had moved on in other ways, tending her roses and returning to the health club and her yoga classes. Last month, she closed Evan's practice and let his secretary go.

She hadn't abandoned hope for Evan's return, but she couldn't deny that her outlook was changing. She was weary of spending nights alone and tired of stressing over finances and her uncertain future. The paperwork held in her hands at least gave her a chance to eliminate one major problem.

Sarah started the engine and allowed cold air to blow

across her face. She closed her eyes and thought about Brian, the man she met in Hawaii. She remembered her childish behavior on the island and their last night together. Walking with him along the beach. Breaking down and crying on his shoulder. She appreciated him for his understanding and compassion. She had gone to his room, although nothing crazy happened. She'd spent the evening sobbing on his bed while he held her and murmured encouragement.

She liked him more after that night.

He accepted the circumstances of her life and understood she was waiting for Evan. Brian made no demands and asked nothing of her. After returning from Hawaii, they began an online relationship. He remained interested and supportive, and lately was floating the idea of Sarah visiting him in San Francisco. The thought tempted her, but she knew such a trip would involve another threshold. If she went to see Brian, she would give in to desire and cross a line. Once over it, she couldn't step back.

She sat in the hot car and leafed through the paperwork. Barring a miracle, next month, the medical examiner would issue a death certificate and she would collect a half-million tax-free dollars from the insurance policy.

She could begin the next phase of her life.

CHAPTER TWENTY-FIVE

Andrea shook him awake.

He heard a buzzing noise as the aircraft passed overhead, flaps down and angled in a landing pattern. Andrea leaped to her feet and dashed into the woods. He grabbed the gear and chased after her, grasping her arm and steering her in the correct direction. Andrea was fit and athletic, running in long strides and breathing easily as she dodged through the trees like a deer. She remained mute as they ran, keeping distance between them and responding to him with nods or shrugs.

After a day of pushing hard, they set up camp amidst a stand of aspens. Nearby, a small waterfall splashed melodically into a shallow pond. He tasked her with searching for firewood, and she returned carrying an armful of branches.

At dusk, she stepped into the shadows. He heard the rustling of clothing, then the splashing of water as she waded into the pond. She moved under the waterfall and again vigorously scrubbed her body. She disappeared into the darkness, and he saw the flare of a match. The odor of marijuana floated his way. He understood what she was doing. Self-medicating. Dulling the pain. When finished, she crawled into the sleeping bag and closed her eyes.

Evan was familiar with the signs of trauma. The bruises and scars on her body would heal. Those left on her soul were another matter. She'd pushed the horror deep into her subconscious mind and wasn't ready to think or feel. He figured she wanted nothing to do with him. Brutalized by inhuman and vile men, she found herself reliant on someone who appeared from nowhere and saved her life. A man. He did not doubt that she felt grateful and terrified of him at the same time. He could only imagine the conflict she must be experiencing and left her alone in her sorrow, allowing her space to travel her path.

Andrea remained distant as they continued their silent trek, but she became increasingly helpful. She spotted a bush of ripe berries and gathered them, offering him a handful. She collected firewood and helped skin and clean game. One evening she fried the venison, and from that day forward she tacitly became the camp cook. She continued her nightly ritual of scrubbing and smoking.

Another day's march, and he set up camp while she went in search of firewood. Slinging the rifle across his shoulder, he walked into the woods. Deer were in abundance and he spotted a grazing pair, heads bent to the grass. He crept close and trained the sights on a good-sized buck. Something alerted the animals, and their heads jerked up. They stared wide-eyed into the trees before bounding away. A moment later, he saw what spooked the deer. A bear. Pushing through the brush, moving in his direction.

It wasn't his grizzly.

A smaller bear, this one a brown sow with twin cubs scampering behind her. The animal moved into the meadow, aggressively swiveling her head and sniffing the air. With no intention of taking on a protective mother and making orphans of her cubs, he stepped behind a tree and monitored the bear's movements. She remained on high alert, standing erect and staring across the meadow. The bear communicated in some way, and her cubs scampered behind a fallen log. They poked heads above it and watched.

The sow continued to perk her ears as she processed forest sounds. Then Evan heard it. Branches breaking. Something moving through the trees, headed in their direction. The bear huffed and dropped to all fours, advancing in stiff-legged hops. It began trotting aggressively towards the intruder.

"Shit," he said.

Andrea stepped into the meadow, her arms filled with firewood as she moved directly into the animal's path.

The bear charged.

Evan shouted and ran towards her.

She spotted the onrushing animal and dropped the wood, running full tilt towards a thick pine tree. She grabbed a low branch and began scrambling up the trunk. The bear was closing fast on her, and Evan could see she wouldn't make it.

He dropped to a knee, raised the rifle and fired. The bear collapsed in a heap, ten feet from the tree. He discharged another round into the animal's body, then ran towards Andrea. She dropped from the tree and fell heavily onto the rough earth.

"Oh God," she said in a voice that was low and hoarse. She allowed him to take her in his arms.

"Thank you," she whispered into his neck.

She pushed him away and wiped tears from her face, then she retrieved the firewood and trudged towards camp. Evan shook his head, mystified. Wondering if angry bears charged her every day. He scanned the woods for the cubs, but they had disappeared. He returned to the sow and began hacking meat from the animal's flank.

She fried the bear steaks, consumed her meal in silence, and washed the skillet in the stream. At nightfall, she engaged in her customary scrubbing before disappearing into the shadows. He poured whiskey into a cup and stared into the fire.

He'd brought down a charging bear with a single shot.

From a full sprint, he'd dropped to his knees, thrown the weapon to his shoulder, and fired without aiming. The slug pierced the animal's heart. A fractional miss and the bear would have torn Andrea to pieces. He shook his head. He couldn't make that shot again if he tried a thousand times.

She emerged from the darkness and joined him by the fire. He pointed to the bottle, and she surprised him by nodding. He found the other cup and poured a generous shot. She raised it to her lips, and for the first time offered a grateful smile.

"You saved my life," she said, "for the second time." Her voice was soft and emotional. "In that camp, you risked your life to rescue me from something worse than death. And today, that bear would have killed me if you hadn't been there."

He smiled and said nothing. He could see that she had more to say.

"I'll never understand how you showed up at the lowest moment of my life. I'll never stop being grateful."

"I'm glad we met," he said. "Happy to have some company out here."

"Sorry I've been distant," she said. "I'll try to be nicer."

"I'd like that," he said. "I've wanted to talk about some things."

"What kind of things?"

"Things I've experienced out here. And I hope you'll tell me about you. You don't have to talk about what happened back there. But I'd like to know how you ended up out here. It might help me figure out some other things. We don't have to talk until you're ready."

"I'm ready," she said.

CHAPTER TWENTY-SIX

"**I**'ll start with the easy part," she said. She winced at the whiskey's bite, then took a long breath. "I teach fifth grade in an inner-city school in Seattle. The job's not easy, but I love it. The classroom. My kids. The challenges. I always believed I was doing something worthwhile. Making a contribution, that kind of thing. But teachers don't get paid a decent salary, and that's the reason I'm in this mess. I finished college four years ago with a degree in elementary education and eighty-five thousand in student loans. The Seattle job was the first offer I got, and I took it. They pay me thirty-two thousand a year, which means I make about fifteen dollars an hour.

"My salary's so far below the poverty line, I qualify for food stamps. I can barely afford groceries. My one-bedroom apartment's a dump and I drive a ten-year-old Mazda. It takes six hundred a month to service the school loan. A cell phone's my only luxury." She picked up a stick and poked the fire, watching a shower of sparks float into the night.

She sighed and shrugged her shoulders. "Sounds like a sob story, I know. But it's part of the reason I ended up out here."

"We have all the time in the world."

She continued to jab at the fire. "Like a lot of teachers, I took on part-time work. Tutoring kids after school. The cosmetics counter in a department store. Most recently, tending bar. None of it paid much more than minimum wage. Every cent went to school loans. After three years of working my ass off, I'd reduced it by a whopping eight thousand dollars. I got sick of it. Thought about changing careers, but an education degree's useless unless you teach. I looked into graduate school, but that would mean more loans, so I gave up that idea pretty quickly. I was stuck in a life I was starting to hate and had no way out.

"A couple of months ago, an old college classmate comes into the bar. She's celebrating, because she'd paid off all her college loans. Cleared off a hundred thousand dollars in less than two years. She started telling me about her part-time job. She worked for an escort service. Once a week, she dressed in heels and a little black dress and accompanied older men to social events. Parties and receptions. Even sporting events. Mostly in Seattle, and once in a while they flew her to Portland or San Francisco."

She extended the cup, and he poured another shot. "The service vetted her clients," she continued, "always sending her older men who were rich and generous. All she had to do was look good. She wasn't a prostitute. There was no sex involved. These men wanted a good-looking woman on their arm when they walked into their event. Most were old and lonely, and they wanted somebody to pay attention to them. Once in a while, somebody got frisky, but they were easy to handle. She made a thousand a night. Plus tips. She drank expensive champagne and ate in five-star restaurants, all on somebody else's tab. I guess she wanted to share her good fortune, because she offered to get me an interview with her boss. A man named Tony Bianchi. The money was tempting, but I turned her down. The idea made me nervous."

Andrea offered him the tiniest smile and shook her head at the idea of her stupidity. "I continued with my crummy little life. Teaching kids all day and pulling evening shifts as a bartender. Then I got laid off from the bar, and the same week my car broke down. The repair bill was four hundred dollars. My credit cards were maxed out and I didn't have that much in my bank account. I was forced to take out a credit union loan." She shook her head at the craziness of it. "I couldn't put my hands on four hundred dollars without taking out a loan. That was the last straw."

She walked to the water's edge and gazed into the night sky before returning to the fire and providing him a grim smile.

"Now comes the hard part," she said. "I called my college friend, and she gave me Bianchi's number. He had a big office on the top floor of a bank building on the waterfront. He's this big overweight Italian guy about forty, with slicked-back hair. Flashy dresser. Wearing a gold Rolex and a big chain around his neck. Obviously filthy rich. He drives around in a Maserati. Owns an airplane. I know he's right out of a Mafia movie, but it never crossed my mind that he wasn't legitimate. His office is in a bank tower. Full of fancy furniture, with secretaries and people in suits running around. He interviewed me for about fifteen minutes. Asked why I wanted the job, and I told him about the loans. Then he asked me to walk around the room. He wanted to see my backside. He apologized, but said I needed to be beautiful and sexy if I wanted to make money. I guess I passed the test. We shook hands, and he said I'd be hearing from him. The next week I got a call. Bianchi told me my friend quit, and I could take her place. I accepted on the spot, and that's how I started my career as a professional escort.

"Right away, the referrals began coming in. Most of the men were nice. A few tried to put moves on me, but they weren't pushy. Some wanted to date me on the side, but the agency discouraged it. I was doing great. Having fun and making a lot of money. I didn't think much about my friend at the time, although now I know what happened to her.

"Overnight, my problems disappeared. I was making a ton of money, and teaching became fun again. I accelerated the loan payments and started thinking about a new car. Then one evening, Bianchi called me. Said he had a business proposition, one that could instantly solve my loan problem. I was excited and couldn't wait to talk to him. He pulled up in a limo, and I got in the back. He didn't come alone. His younger brother Tommy was in the limo. He's the guy you slugged. I got in the limo and they gave me champagne.

"That's the last thing I remember," she said. "I woke up in an airplane."

He could see dark thoughts had entered her head. She looked towards the stars and began breathing rapidly, and then she told him she'd talked enough for the night. She rolled out the sleeping bag and crawled into it.

He stared into the fire until only glowing embers remained. He didn't need to hear any more. He could fill in the rest. He watched her sleeping form and tried to imagine the hell she had endured in that camp, thinking about the depths of human depravity and the evil things that men do.

They spent the next three days climbing the southern slope of a towering mountain. A cap of snow crowned its peak despite the summer heat. They traversed mountain meadows and forested hills, all spectacular in their beauty. Andrea showed no inclination to resume their conversation. Her near-death encounter and fireside talk seemed to release something, and she appeared enthralled by the mountain's majesty. She pointed out a mountain goat perched on a high ledge and marveled at the beauty and peace of the wilderness. She even picked wildflowers and thrust them under his nose.

One evening as they sat by the fire, she extended her cup for whiskey and declared it was his turn to talk. He told her what he remembered of the plane crash and collision with the earth. He described the sad column of bodies, waiting for rescue, and his eventual decision to walk out of the wilderness. He described the mysterious grizzly and his deadly encounter with the wolf pack.

Some things he chose not to reveal. He made no mention of Bigfoot or spaceships. He said nothing of his suicidal leap or miraculous rescue, figuring she would think him insane. Instead, he talked about his life and career. He told her about Sarah and the life he planned when he returned home.

He fell silent, and they stared into the fire.

"There's something I should tell you about these men," she said. "I'm not their first victim. They've abducted other girls. They drug them, fly them out here and have their fun, then kill them. They bragged about it, telling me many women they'd buried near the camp and promising me I'd join them. I think my friend might be one of them."

"Who are they?"

"Drug people," she said. "Part of some big cartel. I heard them talking about it. They're filthy rich, and they don't make it from running an escort service. I think they use it to launder drug money. And these people are brutal. They talked about murdering me like it's a game. They were going to turn me loose into the woods. They made a bet who'd hunt me down and shoot me first."

"Didn't they figure somebody would come looking for you?"

"I'm convinced they use the service to identify vulnerable women. I live alone, and I'm new to the area. I don't have a boyfriend. I don't teach during the summer. If I disappeared, not many people would miss me. I guess I fit their profile."

"The one flying the airplane, you said he's the older brother?"

She nodded. "Tony Bianchi. The big boss. He runs the operation. He set up their little camp of horrors. He's probably looking for me right now. I know what he's done. Where the bodies are buried. And he'll be crazy for revenge after what you did to his brother. He'll come after you, too."

"This is a big place. They won't find us."

"Don't be so sure," she said.

CHAPTER TWENTY-SEVEN

Traveling became easier as they began their descent down the backside of the mountain. The cloud-shrouded peaks of yet another range came into view, filling the western sky and obstructing their intended route. He unfolded the map and decided a southerly passage would provide more favorable terrain.

Andrea continued to emerge from her shell, becoming more talkative and interested in the world around her. He figured she had buried the ghastly memories and emotions inside her mind, although he caught an occasional glimpse of it. A distant look in her eyes. Startling at a clattering skillet or rustling in the woods. Jerking away if he approached too suddenly. Her continued nightly rituals of body cleansing and weed smoking.

They stopped to rest beneath the shade of a massive tree. He was studying the map, attempting to fix their location. Andrea was twirling a dandelion and staring at a grass-filled meadow across the valley.

"Something's over there," she said, motioning for the binoculars.

"What are you seeing?"

"Bear. Big one."

"White patch on its rump?"

"Yup," she said. "Your friend?"

"Must be," he said. "How many bears have a white spot on their rear end?"

"Why would a big old grizzly want to follow you?"

"I wish he'd tell us," he said, "because I don't have a clue." She tracked the bear through the glasses until it disappeared through a notch in the mountain.

It was late afternoon when they arrived at the bank of a fast-running river. The current crashed into enormous boulders, throwing spray high into the air and transforming the river into foaming rapids. Crossing it was an impossibility, so they turned upriver to seek calmer waters. The river grew louder as they moved upstream, and a tall waterfall came into view.

A massive wall of water fell from a granite cliff, crashing into a crystal-clear pond and bouncing high into the air. A multihued rainbow arched above the water, shimmering and incandescent in the misty air. The pond was beautiful and pristine, and below the surface they could see darting shadows of fish.

Andrea insisted they camp beside the waterfall.

There was daylight to burn, but he capitulated without argument and dropped the backpack. Pointing towards the pond, he announced trout would be on the dinner menu. He began a search for earthworms while Andrea went off to collect firewood. He set up the rod and cast a line, pulling out a pair of wriggling rainbows.

Andrea stood beside the cascading waters, stretching her arms and raising her head towards the sky. She appeared opaque and ethereal as the disappearing sun backlit her body and sparkling mist rose around her. He watched her shimmering image and for a moment thought she was floating above the water. She disappeared behind the cascading falls and emerged a minute later, motioning for him to join her. He stepped behind the waterfall and followed as she ran down a narrow ledge cut into the mountainside. She stopped and pointed to a fissure carved from the granite wall.

Nature's hand had scooped an elongated cavity into the side of the mountain. The cave floor was smooth stone, and the ceiling thick with pale stalactites. Walls damp and mossy from the waterfall's mist glittered with reflected light. Evan flipped on the flashlight and shone it towards the back of the cave.

He knew from his country roots that wild creatures tended to inhabit dark places. Bats, bears or snakes found homes in caves, although he could see no sign of such habitation. There was evidence of human occupation. An ancient circle of fire-blackened rocks arranged in the middle of the stone floor. Remnants of animal skin. Cave walls adorned with crude drawings of people and animals, maybe deer and bear.

Andrea was enchanted.

Camping beside the pond was deemed too ordinary, and it became imperative that they spend the night in this cave. He grumbled a bit but fetched the gear and hauled up an armload of wood, building a fire while Andrea set up the sleeping bags. She held a tin cup beneath the waterfall and drank, then extended it to him. The water tasted cold and delicious.

They dined on trout fried over the fire, and after dinner she left the cave and returned an hour later with glistening hair and the smell of marijuana. She accepted the proffered cup of bourbon and began walking around the cave, gazing at the gallery of crude drawings.

"Never imagined I'd be camping in a prehistoric cave a million miles from nowhere," she said, "drinking booze by a campfire."

He chuckled. "Like it?"

She nodded enthusiastically. "This place is like something from a Disney movie."

She rummaged through her backpack and held up the baggie. She rolled a fat joint and wet it with her tongue, then she fired up the thing and took a long drag. She held up the joint and showed it to him.

"Ever try it?"

He shook his head. "Not weed. But I did other stuff in college."

Her eyes widened in surprise. "You were a druggie?"

"Not really. As an undergrad, I took part in a drug study." He smiled and arched his brows mischievously. "Strictly for research purposes, of course."

"Okay, I'll bite. What drug?"

"LSD, believe it or not."

"You dropped acid in college? Get outta here."

"It wasn't about fun and recreation. One of my professors had this brilliant theory that LSD could alleviate psychiatric symptoms. He set up a study and recruited his students for the control group."

Andrea seemed amused by the idea that he'd used a hallucinogenic drug. "I love it," she said. "You tripped on acid. Did you get high?"

"Oh, yeah," he said. "It was interesting. Hard to describe. I had flashbacks the entire semester. Kept seeing these weird geometric patterns and flashing lights."

"Crazy," she said. "So you've dropped acid but never smoked weed?"

He shook his head. "Too strait-laced in high school and too serious in college. It was illegal back then, and I didn't want to go to jail. When I became a psychologist, I had to pass random drug tests and wasn't interested in losing my license. But I've always been curious. Marijuana's on my list of things to try someday."

"What state are we in right now?"

He shrugged. "Oregon. Or Washington."

She extended the joint. "Either way, it's legal in both places. Care to cross one off your bucket list?"

"Why not," he said. He held the joint between finger and thumb. "Not sure what to do with it."

She giggled. "Same as your cigar. Take a hit off it and hold the smoke in your lungs, then exhale and enjoy the sensation. Repeat the procedure, then hand the doobie back to me. That's all there is to it."

He did as instructed, then held up the joint to examine it.

"How am I supposed to be feeling?"

"This cave is a perfect place for your first experience. We're surrounded by nature and feeling relaxed, so you'll probably get a mellow buzz. You might need a few more hits before you feel anything."

They talked while passing the joint back and forth. She rolled another one and lay on the sleeping bag, studying the haze of smoke drifting towards the ceiling.

"All we need is music to make it perfect," she said.

He opened his backpack and rummaged through it. "Here you go," he said. He tossed her a cell phone. "See what you can find in there."

She gave him a curious look. "This thing work?"

"We can't call anybody if that's what you mean," he said. "No signal. But there's a music icon on the lock screen. You can play tunes without unlocking it."

"You don't want to save the battery?"

"I've got phones."

She activated it and found the icon, clicking it open and scrolling through a song list. "Bingo," she said.

"You got tunes?"

"Whoever owned this phone liked sixties music." She hit a button, and the sounds of Jefferson Airplane began bouncing off cave walls.

"Perfect weed music," she said.

"All of a sudden, the lyrics make sense."

She giggled and took another hit.

"You seem to know what you're doing," he said.

"Oh, yeah. I'm familiar with the concept of weed." She pulled a drag into her lungs, releasing it with a laugh. "I got high in college, mostly at parties, and stopped using when I started working. Didn't want to get fired. Now it's different. Marijuana's legal these days, even for teachers. You just can't get high at school. Besides, at the moment I'm a million miles from my classroom. Sitting in a cave. No phone. No internet. No cable. Just a baggie of weed. It's the entertainment of choice."

He gestured for the joint and took a drag, watching as smoke drifted upwards and insinuated itself among stalactites. Enjoying the relaxing effects of cannabis and psychedelic music, his mind shifted into a contemplative mood. He watched as Andrea began swaying to the music. The Doors. "Light My Fire" reverberated through the cave. Her lips pantomimed the song's words as she twirled and danced towards the cave wall.

She made an infinite adjustment in posture and her figure shifted in some way. She turned her body in profile and transformed into someone else. No longer the listless and defeated trauma victim. Now she was an alluring woman in full sexual prime. Her profile in firelight revealed abundant breasts straining against her shirt, and the flat tummy and full hips enhanced her sexuality.

The rush of lustful thoughts heated him like a furnace. It wasn't the first time he'd experienced this visceral reaction to her. He'd caught moonlit flashes of her body when she engaged in her bathing ritual. As he watched her sway, he felt the urgent desire to grind his body against hers.

He told himself it was a natural reaction. They were a man and woman marooned in the wilderness, far from home and reliant on one another for survival. More than once he had saved her life, and she was helping him navigate the forest. In the evening, they sat by the fire and talked, growing closer as they learned more about one another. Sometimes their trek through the wilds had the feel of an adventure, and lately they were even having fun. Chasing butterflies and smoking weed, engaging in a relationship that was intimate in every way but sexual.

He watched her sensuous movements, indulging in the fantasy of pulling her into his sleeping bag and climbing atop her. After a while, he exhaled heavily and pushed the lascivious thoughts from his mind. There was a formidable age gap between them, and she hadn't given the slightest indication of romantic interest in him. Besides, cheating wasn't in his makeup. He was still loyal to Sarah, despite her betrayal of him, and Andrea was a vulnerable trauma victim. The last thing she needed was a sexual advance from a man she was only beginning to trust. They would smoke marijuana and listen to music.

That would be it.

"When do you think these drawings were made?" Andrea said.

"They look ancient," he said. "I'd guess at least a hundred years ago."

"The artist made do with what he found here. I'll bet he used mud from the pond to create his masterpieces," she said. "He mixed in something to make it glitter and used his fingers as a brush. He drew a little family. The taller figures are the stick mom and dad, and the little one's a stick kid."

She ran a hand over the crude drawings. "It's awesome to think somebody passed through this area so long ago and stayed in this cave. They slept by this fire. The artist was so inspired that he left behind a record. I wonder who they were and what they were doing here. Where were they going?"

"On their own journey, I guess."

This seemed to give her an idea. She disappeared through the mouth of the cave and returned with handfuls of mud. She held up the dripping muck so he could see it and offered a mischievous smile.

"Let's leave our mark," she said. "I'll draw you, and you draw me."

They found a bare spot and added their figures to the gallery.

He watched as she drew a figure. The line of mud representing his body was strong and thick, his arms thrust upwards. A large head and dots for eyes and nose, and a smiling face. He dipped his hand into the mud and drew a smaller figure standing beside him. He gave her an oval face with a big half-circle of a smile and drew lines from her head to represent hair. She finished their creation by drawing the letters A and E beneath their figures. She connected the letters with a big plus sign. She stood back and examined their work. He could see she liked it.

"We're quite the artists," he said.

"The next visitors will know we were here," she said, and he smiled in agreement. She looked around the cave.

"I'm in love with this place," she declared. "Let's stay here forever. We can live in this cave and have adventures."

"It's a deal." He gave her a playful smile. "We just need more weed."

She held up the baggie and grinned. "I've got seeds."

They smoked more grass and chattered like teenagers on a campout, talking about favorite movies and television shows. Bands and concerts. Dream vacations. They listened to more songs, then lay in the darkness listening to the fire's crackling embers. He became fascinated with the dancing shadows cast by the firelight. Andrea lit another joint and stared at its glowing end.

"Something's happening here," she said.

"What it is ain't exactly clear?"

She slugged him on the shoulder. "Funny," she said. "I'm serious."

He rose onto an elbow. "What's happening?"

"This place. These woods. It feels strange. I'm not talking weed buzz. It's something else. Sometimes I feel like I'm watching myself through someone else's eyes. I wonder if this is a dream."

"Am I in your dream, or are you in mine?"

"Now that's weed talk," she said.

He got serious. "I know what you mean. It does sometimes feel odd. Dreamlike, I guess. There's something I can't bring into focus. Information I should know. It's at the edge of my mind, but I can't quite grasp it."

"Sometimes when I close my eyes, it feels like I'm not here."

"Where are you?"

"I don't know," she said. "Just not here. And my sense of time's all messed up. How long you figure you've been out here?"

"You mean since the crash?"

She nodded.

"I don't know," he said. "A few weeks, I think. But sometimes it feels like I've been traipsing through these woods for years."

"I know, right?" she said.

They lay in silence, listening to the popping of embers. He understood what she was experiencing. Things seemed peculiar in a way he couldn't identify or articulate. Slightly out of focus or surreal. The thought slipped away as he drifted back into the marijuana buzz.

"You believe in miracles?" she said.

"Another weed-based question?"

"Probably, she said. "But something I've been thinking about."

"I watched an eagle floating in the sky one day," he said. "It was circling, way up in the clouds. All of a sudden, this eagle dove straight down and snatched a rabbit. Pulled it high into the air before the rabbit shook loose and dropped to the ground. I thought the thing was dead, but it jumped up and ran away." He raised his palms and shrugged. "Did I witness a miracle? Or was the rabbit lucky that day?"

Andrea contemplated the joint before taking a drag. "You answered my question with a question."

"Well," he said, "I walked away from an airplane crash that killed sixteen men," he said. "That's a miracle by anybody's definition."

She extended the joint and he took it. "You said other weird things have happened out here. Care to share?"

He thought about it before shaking his head. "I don't want you thinking I'm nuts. Anyway, returning to the topic of miracles. Your thoughts?"

"Never believed in such things," she said, pausing to offer him a smile. "Now I'm not so sure. Your presence in my life definitely constitutes a miracle."

"Ditto," he said.

They fell silent and passed the joint until it was done, and the weed buzz and waterfall sounds lulled them to sleep. The cave reeked of marijuana when they awoke, and he teased her about getting him high.

They loaded their gear and continued their journey.

Andrea kept a close eye on the skies as they continued their westward trek.

He knew what she was doing.

Watching for an airplane. Keeping an eye out for Tony Bianchi. She stood atop a small knoll and shaded her eyes as she inspected the sky, then she ran the glasses down the trail behind them. Apparently satisfied, she trained the binoculars on the valley ahead.

"Come here," she said. "You need to see this."

She handed him the glasses and directed him to a creek that wound along the valley's southern edge along the foot of a mountain. "Follow that creek upstream, to where it curves into the woods. There's a pond at the bend. Tell me what you see."

He found the stream and followed its path. The creek was narrow, its waters reflecting sunlight back into his eyes. Blinking at the glare, he tracked the stream until it emptied into a little pond. He turned to stare at her.

"A cabin," he said.

CHAPTER TWENTY-EIGHT

A young altar boy held a golden cross aloft and led the procession through the nave of the cavernous church. The white-haired priest followed, wearing a bright green cassock and singing an entrance hymn in a cultured baritone voice. An elderly deacon trailed the priest, carrying the Evangelion that contained the holy gospel. More altar boys followed behind, carrying blessed candles. The last boy in the procession carried an incense-filled thurible, swinging the smoking vessel a bit too enthusiastically. The priest genuflected as he kissed the altar, then he turned to the congregation and made the sign of the cross.

"He'll invite us to take part in the penitential act," Rose whispered. "Just follow along and say amen when everybody else does." Sarah watched as her friend's hands moved busily along a strand of rosary beads. Rose was dressed for Sunday Mass, wearing a colorful cotton dress that extended to her ankles, low heels, and a lace mantilla veil. The ever-present wooden cross hung around her neck, and her face held a beatific smile as the processional moved past their pew.

Today's service was nearly identical to ones Sarah had attended over the past several weeks. The ritualized readings from Hebrew scriptures, the letters of Paul, and the four Gospels. Then the homily, to help the congregation understand the relevance of the scriptures to everyday life. The congregation repeatedly prayed, sang, and knelt. Sarah tuned out much of it, growing restless as Rose joined the line for communion. Then more hymns were sung. Another string of prayers. It was all Sarah could do to stay seated as the priest blessed and dismissed the congregation. Finally, Mass was over.

They adjourned to Rose's house for brunch and wine. Sarah had found Rose to be a kindred spirit. Both their husbands were victims of the air crash, and Rose was someone who understood the depths of her loss. They'd formed a support group of sorts. Just the two of them getting together every week to talk about their lost men. Helping one another cope with the colossal void in their lives and navigating a path past the pain. Rose was devout, and her answer was simple. God would heal her. An impassioned believer, she was intent on sharing with Sarah the healing powers of God's love. She eventually convinced Sarah to accompany her to Mass.

Religion had never been a part of Sarah's life. She'd

grown up in an upper-middle-class family. Her father an engineer, her mother a math teacher. Rational thinking was the family religion, and logic the homily. Her parents didn't attend church and didn't force religion on her. Sarah met Evan in college, and they were like-minded in many ways. Both open to the concept of a higher power, but neither comfortable with the idea of organized religion or ritualized worship. They'd been content to leave unanswered their questions about God's existence. Then Evan's plane went down and her world imploded, and now she was searching for answers.

"Better today?" Rose asked.

Sarah smiled. "I don't mind going with you. I like the pageantry and the smell of myrrh and frankincense. But I'm not sure church is the answer for me."

Rose hesitated, as if trying to decide whether to say something. "You're carrying a heavy burden," she said. "God can help you with it."

"I miss my husband," Sarah said. "Just like you."

"Something more is bothering you. I can see the pain in your eyes. Maybe you blame yourself for what's happened to Evan. I know I felt that way for a while. Maybe it's something else. Whatever's troubling you, it's tearing at your soul and robbing you of peace." Rose's eyes were filled with compassion as she raised placating hands. "You don't have to talk to me about it. But you should tell somebody."

"God, I suppose?" Sarah felt irritation heat her face. She didn't want to travel this road with Rose. She wasn't interested in sharing her shame and reopening painful wounds. Mostly, she was sick of hearing about God.

"His compassion is infinite," Rose said. "Whatever you've done, God already knows. What can it hurt to ask his forgiveness?" She rummaged in her purse for a Bible. "There's a verse I want to read you."

"Don't," Sarah said, raising a hand.

Rose appeared puzzled. "It's an inspirational reading about God's boundless love and compassion."

"I'm sorry, but I've had my fill of God." She saw the hurt flare in Rose's eyes but couldn't stop herself as the emotional floodgates burst open. "I know you mean well. But you're shoving God down my throat. You believe in him. I get it. But I feel differently. For me, God's an unproven theory. I don't even understand the concept. How can people worship a deity who does nothing but inflict pain and suffering? Why pray to a God that tolerates disasters and catastrophes, allows children to contract diseases and tolerates mass murderers? What kind of all-loving God would take from us the people we love most?"

"God doesn't reveal his plan," Rose said. "He asks us to believe in his wisdom, and that's the essence of faith. His ways are mysterious. But I trust in him and I know he loves you. What can it hurt to talk to him? He understands what you've lost. Remember, he gave up his only son for us." She grasped the cross on her neck and brought it to her lips.

Her naïve piety only served to piss off Sarah even more. "That's another thing that doesn't make any sense. God loves us so much that he allowed Christ to be nailed to a cross, mutilated and tortured? Really? Wasn't there something else he could have done? Something less cruel and horrible? And Jesus supposedly was resurrected, in case you forgot. If this God you worship is so wonderful, why doesn't he do the same for Evan and Gene?"

"I didn't mean to upset you," Rose said. Her face flushed, and tears swam in her eyes. She came to Sarah and they hugged, and soon both were crying. The tears washed away Sarah's anger, and now she just felt sad and lonely.

"I'm the one who needs to apologize to you," she said. "I didn't intend to disparage your beliefs. Please don't stop sharing your faith with me. I've just been so angry lately. At everybody. Myself. Evan. The world in general. I want to move on and get back to living, but I can't seem to find a way."

"I'm sorry for pushing my beliefs onto you," Rose said. "I hoped that finding God might help you release your pain. For me, the church is a place of renewal and peace. I was hoping it would be the same for you."

"It doesn't work that way for me. I feel like such a hypocrite any time I step inside a church."

"Why would you feel that way?"

"I've never attended church. Never prayed. Now my life's a disaster and I'm supposed to beg God to take away my pain?"

"What else is there for you?"

"I don't know," Sarah said. "Family, I guess. Friends. Work. You."

They fell quiet, and Rose poured more wine. "Waking up each morning without my Gene," she said, "is the hardest thing I've ever done. He's constantly in my mind. But with God's love, I've found peace and acceptance."

Sarah rose and walked to the mezuzah hanging near a doorway. "So delicate and beautiful," she murmured. "Why's it slanted this way?"

"I guess the old Rabbis couldn't decide whether to hang the mezuzah vertically or horizontally, so they compromised." Rose extended a hand and touched the ornament, then she kissed her fingers. "We touch it to remind ourselves that God is everywhere and to live a spiritual life."

"You're more Catholic than the Pope but have this Jewish charm in your house. You are a fascinating person."

Rose smiled and shrugged. "Doesn't hurt to cover all your bases."

Sarah exhaled wearily. "I'm tired of hurting. I want to start living again."

"You will," Rose said, "and I want to be there when you do. For now, I'll stop dragging you to church and cool it with the God talk. But I want to give you something." She handed Sarah a tiny box. It held a small gold cross and chain.

"It's beautiful," Sarah said, holding the cross up to the light. She carefully returned it to the box and leaned to hug her friend.

"I hope you'll one day wear it," Rose said. "It will remind you of God's love and give you strength."

"Maybe one day I'll feel that way," Sarah said.

CHAPTER TWENTY-NINE

"I've never seen anything so beautiful," Andrea said.

They stood at the edge of a pristine meadow covered in lush green grass so uniform that it appeared freshly mowed. Wildflowers grew in abundance, hummingbirds busy among them, and the chirping of birds filled the air. The circumference of the meadow was ringed with rows of trees heavy with fruit.

On the far side of the meadow, they discovered a garden overgrown with tall weeds. Spindly stalks of corn rose from the undergrowth. On the ground lay a network of vines flush with tomatoes. A crooked row of watermelon ripened in the sun, and a variety of vegetables grew in wild profusion.

A sluice channel cut from the creek fed the garden. Another ditch returned the water to a sparkling pond that rippled with fish. Near the cabin was dug a fire pit made of smooth embedded river rock. A rusted pot dangled from a rough-welded iron stand straddling the pit, and beside it stood a rickety picnic table.

Evan was staring at the cabin. "This place is ancient."

Constructed with hand-cut pine logs now weathered and grayed, gaps caulked with river mud and straw, the place still looked sturdy and habitable. Once forest green, the paint was now curled and faded. Crude hand-made shutters covered a rough-cut rectangular window hole, and an old door had fallen away from rusted hinges. A crooked stove pipe poked from the pitched roof.

He wrenched open the rickety door, pushing aside a curtain of cobwebs as he stepped inside and ran a flashlight around the cabin's dark interior. He carefully tested the floor before venturing further into the room. He pushed away rotted shutters, and sunlight illuminated the room's interior. He signaled to Andrea, and she cautiously followed him into the cabin. The place consisted of a single rectangular room, perhaps twenty by twenty feet. No running water or indoor plumbing. The walls and ceiling were unfinished, the floor constructed of rough planks that groaned with their weight.

Furniture consisted of a weather-beaten split pine table and narrow cot. A pair of folding camp chairs. A melted candle sat in the middle of the table. Beside it, an open book and grimy beer bottle. A wad of bedding piled in one corner and a rusted stove squatted in another, its pipe corroded and collapsed. Uneven plank shelves were stacked high with paperbacks. The only wall décor was a map affixed with thumbtacks. A stack of wooden boxes occupied another corner. Cobwebs and dust covered every surface of the room. A dusty kerosene lamp hung from a wall hook.

Evan took shook his head at the sight. "Who'd build a place in the middle of nowhere? And why?"

"Coulda' been a hunter's cabin," she said. "Or trappers from a long time ago. Maybe a survivalist living off the grid." She shrugged as she gazed around the cabin. "Could be somebody running from the law."

"Or a novelist trying to create his version of Walden," he said. He examined thick pine logs used to construct the walls. They were solidly braced, with bolts and heavy nails holding everything together.

"I wonder if it was our stick family."

He gave her a puzzled look.

"The people who drew their portraits on the cave wall."

"Possible, but not likely," he said. "Whoever built this didn't just hike out here and start chopping down trees. Putting this place together took planning and organization, and it wasn't built overnight. They had to get building materials to this site, and there's no sign of a road or runway. I can't imagine how they did it."

He pulled the map from the wall and carried it outside, where he sat at the picnic table and studied it. "This is interesting," he said.

She was staring over his shoulder. "What's interesting?"

"What's drawn on this map."

He pointed to a series of circled spots on the map, then ran his eyes across the mountains surrounding the valley. He tapped the map with a finger. "This circle marks the cabin's location. The other ones identify bearing points that orient you to its location. This cabin's sitting in a good-sized valley flanked by two mountain ranges."

Evan pointed towards the tall mountain to the north. "The twin peaks atop that mountain provide one bearing point. We can't see it for the trees, but in that direction there's another mountain with a rock fissure that splits it down the middle. This cabin is located squarely between the two mountains."

"Okay, I get it," she said, sounding a trifle impatient. "You line up bearing points on the two mountains and draw a line between them, you'll be able to find the cabin." She gave him a quizzical look. "What's the big deal? We don't need to know how to find this place. We're already here."

"Good point," he said, smiling as he moved his finger to another spot on the map. "Here's the big deal."

He ran a finger along another line, this one jagged and drawn in faded red pencil. The route began at the cabin and wove serpentine-like through the forest. The line continued to a good-sized river, where it jogged sharply to the north and connected to another circle drawn around a town's name.

"This is our ticket home," he said, whooping in excitement as he jumped to his feet and waved the map like a winning lottery ticket. "There's a town not far away, and this map shows us how to get there." He fidgeted as he gazed at the afternoon sun. "It's probably too late to head out today. We leave at first light, and we'll be sitting in our living rooms in a couple of days." He stopped his little victory dance as he saw emotions ripple across Andrea's face.

"Here's the thing," she said, her voice soft and tentative. "We just got here, and this meadow is beautiful. So peaceful. Can we stay a couple of days? Maybe explore the place and rest up a little."

His face flushed in irritation as he fought the impulse to ask if she was crazy. Only the fading sunlight stopped him from dashing into the woods right now. Home was tantalizing close, an easy three-day hike from this spot, and Andrea was suddenly in no hurry to get there. It pissed him off, but his frustration vanished when he saw the fear in her eyes.

A nightmare awaited her in the city. She would carry home the humiliation and torture inflicted out here. Police reports would be filed, and investigations undertaken. The media would want to know her story. There would be court appearances and testimony. She would live her life in fear of retribution from the

Bianchi's. Evan gazed at the bucolic meadow and understood why she was reluctant to leave.

They'd been in the woods a long time. One more day wouldn't matter.

"Okay," he said. "One day, then we head for home."

She rewarded him with a radiant smile of relief. They set up camp and slept beneath the stars, lying near one another beside the fire. Morning greeted them with sparkling sun and the chirping of birds. They spent hours exploring their surroundings. The garden was bursting with vegetables, fruit trees were heavy with succulent treasures, and trout splashed in the pond. He burned the rickety picnic table for firewood and dragged from the cabin the old table and chairs. Andrea cut wildflowers and stuffed them in an antique Coca Cola bottle.

She spent the morning in the garden, digging out the overgrown furrows. At lunchtime, she walked through the meadow carrying something in her arms. She smiled and held out what she'd found -- a tiny gray creature with big eyes and ears lay trembling in her arms. The baby rabbit was far too young to fend for itself, and she held it close to her breast.

"No sign of its mother," she said with a shy smile. "I think it's been abandoned, so I'm going to take care of it."

He considered trying to convince her otherwise, but instead he cobbled together a pen from old boards.

She fashioned a little bed from a sheet, fed the bunny garden greens, and took to carrying the animal with her. He watched with interest as she harvested edibles from the garden and tenderly cared for the tiny rabbit. Good therapy, he figured. By growing things and focusing on new life, she was distancing herself from the trauma. Andrea stroked the little rabbit and gazed across the meadow.

"I could stay here," she said.

"You're getting your way," he said. "We're staying another day."

"I mean forever."

He chuckled. "I thought you wanted to live in a cave."

"Well, this could be our main house and the cave could be our hideout. We live here most of the time and hide in the cave if somebody's chasing after us. I love this place. It's so safe and peaceful."

He realized she was serious. "Living here would take hard work," he said. "It requires knowledge and experience we don't possess."

"We can get the knowledge," she said, "because whoever built this place left us instructions." She dashed into the cabin, returning with two dusty paperbacks.

"I found them on the shelf. This one tells you how to plant a garden. The other book's about wilderness living. It tells you what kinds of plants are safe to eat, how to figure out north from south, and stuff like that." She leafed through the book while they finished lunch, pointing out interesting information.

"If you draw a line between the two points of a crescent moon, the line points to the south," she read aloud. "You can also determine direction by using the hands of your watch or making a solar compass. Blue and black-colored berries are usually safe to eat. Lighter colored ones are probably poisonous so you should never eat them. Persimmons and black walnuts grow in this region. The walnuts fall off the trees, and you hunt for them on the ground. They look like green tennis balls."

After a while, she put down the book and wandered back to the garden, carrying the little rabbit with her While she tended to the vegetable patch, Evan began investigating the riddle of the cabin. Who had possessed the skills and resources to construct this place in such a remote location? What was their reason?

He walked the perimeter of the meadow and discovered an overgrown path. He followed it to a clearing filled with gray stumps, which he squatted to inspect. No hand ax had felled these trees. Someone used a chain saw and possessed a considerable degree of skill in using it. He spotted the rusted saw buried in a rotted log, a dented and a corroded fuel can lay nearby. Scattered about were the remains of broken pallets, desiccated packing straps, and weathered remnants of packing materials.

He examined the scattered detritus, before returning to the cabin. He walked past the rabbit pen, now holding two bunnies. He wondered if mother rabbits were scampering through the garden in search of their babies.

Andrea was enjoying the garden. It was apparent the patch hadn't been tended in decades, but vegetables sprouted in abundance. Rows of carrots, cucumber, and tomatoes, all ripe for picking. Onions and potatoes, watermelon, and corn. The adjacent orchard was also in full bloom. Apples and peaches grew in abundance. Andrea plucked the ripe fruit and filled a canvas bag she'd found in the cabin.

An old hoe rested against one of the trees, its wooden handle cracked and splintered. She took the tool into the garden and spent the afternoon clearing weeds from furrows and digging out the water channel.

Growing weary from her labors, she threw down the hoe and returned to explore the cabin. She found little of interest on the shelves, which held dozens of yellowed books of pulp fiction. Whoever built this place was a fan of John McDonald and Lawrence Sanders, writers she didn't recognize. In the corner lay an old bag of flour torn open and filled with black bugs. A row of cans without labels. A rusted and cracked mirror. All of it junk, but her search wasn't a complete bust. She pried open a box and found a cache of bourbon. She pulled down a dusty bottle and set it aside.

She turned her attention to the crates. Like everything else in the place, they were desiccated and covered in dust. She pried open the first one and removed a canvas knapsack, once tan but now black with age. She brushed away the dust and unbuckled the leather straps, pulling back the flap.

Her brows arched in surprise when she saw what the bag contained.

CHAPTER THIRTY

"Something unusual happened out here," Evan said.

He threw a chunk of wood onto the fire and watched the burst of sparks jump into the night. He was puffing on a cigar and sipping whiskey salvaged from the cabin. A half-century-old, the booze tasted smooth and aged. The evening was fresh and fragrant, filled with the faint scent of roses. A chorus of croaking bullfrogs rose in serenade from the pond.

"Like what?" Andrea gazed at the glowing end of a joint. She exhaled and a plume of smoke drifted into the air.

"Don't know," he said. "Probably something bad. A solitary man built this cabin. I'm thinking he wanted to hide from somebody or something. Then he just abandoned it. Took off in a hurry."

"And you know this because…..?"

"The way he left the cabin. A skillet on the stove. Dried up coffee in a cup. An open book on the table."

"Makes sense, I suppose," she said. She held the

joint to his lips, and he took a drag. "You're sure one dude did all this?"

"We found a single razor and toothbrush in the cabin. One sleeping bag and a solitary set of utensils."

"Okay, one guy built the place. Then he took off. You figure out how he did it? Or why he abandoned it?"

"I've figured out the first part. He set up a logistics chain, operating out of Seattle or Portland. He was a pilot or hired one because he airlifted everything out here. He dropped in a ton of gear —bags of concrete, a crate of tools, nails, caulking, a wheelbarrow, a chain saw. A pallet of food and supplies. That little stove in the cabin. The bed. Another pallet carried materials for the garden – seeds, fertilizer."

Evan pointed through the woods, towards an adjacent meadow. "He culled logs from over there. Felled his trees with the chain saw, then trimmed and skinned them before skidding the logs over here. Each log had to weigh a ton, so he set up a system of winches -- you can see gouges in trees along the dragline. He hand-dug footers with a shovel and mixed concrete in the wheelbarrow. He rigged a pulley and rope system to lift the logs into place, notching them with the chain saw. He assembled this place like Lincoln Logs, and it's stout. He built this place for the long haul."

"He planted a garden and fruit trees, so he meant to

stay awhile," Andrea said. "The question is, why did he do it? And why did he leave?"

"Not a clue."

"I might have one." It was evident that she had been awaiting her turn at show and tell. She smiled and ducked into the cabin, returning with a canvas knapsack. She dropped the bag at his feet.

"Here's a clue for you."

He pulled back the flap and looked into the bag. His eyes widened in surprise. He dumped it, and out tumbled bundles of cash bound with paper wrappers.

"My God," he said. He raised his eyes to hers. "How much?"

"A hundred and ninety-four thousand dollars." She giggled in excitement. "I counted it three times already. All twenties, a hundred of them in each bundle. Each bundle's two thousand bucks. There are ninety-seven bundles."

"Where'd you find it?"

"In a box covered in cobwebs."

"Crazy," he said. "He left behind all this money. Wish we knew more about him."

Andrea snapped her fingers and jumped to her feet. "I found something else in that box. Might give us some answers." She hurried into the cabin and returned with an oversized manila envelope.

"I found this alongside the knapsack," she said.

"You look inside?"

"Too busy counting cash."

She frowned and cocked her head. "Hear that?"

Buzzing sounds echoed through the woods. He ran for the binoculars and raised them to his eyes. Blinking aircraft lights moved slowly across the sky.

"Put out the fire." Andrea's voice was high-pitched with fear.

He doused the fire while Andrea shivered and stared into the sky until the lights disappeared into the night.

"It was high up," he said. "Unlikely that anyone spotted us."

She offered an apologetic smile. "I heard the noise and panicked. I'm fine now."

"You sure?"

"It was a stupid airplane. No biggie. Let's get back to our mystery."

Evan yawned and stretched. "It's late," he said. "Let's put off our sleuthing until the morning."

"We're staying longer?"

"A day or two," he said. "Let's figure this out. Then we'll go home."

CHAPTER THIRTY-ONE

Tony Bianchi made an initial pass above the little cabin, then he rolled the Cessna into a turn and maneuvered the craft into a lower altitude flyover while the man beside him studied the ground.

"Whatta we got?" Bianchi said.

The man squinted as he peered through the binoculars. "Two people next to a campfire. A man and woman."

"Got the assholes," Bianchi growled as he thumped a fist against the console, and his fleshy face creased into a satisfied smile.

Bianchi's body had thickened from years of indulgent living and rich food, and he could barely squeeze himself into the Cessna's narrow seat. Coarse black hair covered every millimeter of his body except his head, which he kept shaven, and he sported a goatee speckled with gray. Despite his bulk and the meaty hands gripping the Cessna's controls, Bianchi was a skilled pilot experienced at night flying.

He'd begun his career as an airborne drug mule, ferrying bundles of cocaine from southern Jalisco to a dirt runway outside San Bernardino. He dropped his loads at an obscure building in the warehouse district that served as the heart of a network of arteries pumping tons of hard drugs through Southern California. Most of the junk the Hollywood elite shoved up their noses was delivered courtesy of Tony Bianchi. A skilled and fearless pilot, Bianchi was unafraid to take chances and adept at evading detection. It was risky work for him and highly profitable for the cartel.

His skills earned him the opportunity to carry bigger payloads, and soon Bianchi was hauling four million dollars' worth of cocaine into California every month. His bosses made billions and Bianchi rose swiftly through the ranks, learning the drug business along the way. This included an understanding that murder was an efficient way of solving problems. It helped considerably that Bianchi was a psychopath who enjoyed inflicting pain. He found sadistic satisfaction as someone begged for their life while he held a pistol to their head. Those proclivities found their way into his sexual interests, and they were the reason he was wasting time right now instead of running his business.

The mess he needed to clean up began a year ago, when Bianchi became obsessed with a stripper, a gorgeous Latina with a powerhouse body, the athleticism of a gymnast, and the face of an angel. A nice girl with a boyfriend and a day job, she dreamed of getting married and having kids. She stripped on the side, putting away her money for a down payment on a home. Bianchi lusted for her the instant he saw her naked body gyrating around the stripper pole, and he began fantasizing about dominating her.

She had no interest in him. A rare woman of scruples among those who removed their clothes for money, she wouldn't sleep with Bianchi and told him so in her sassy Latina way. The rejection infuriated Bianchi, making him crazier for her. When he could stand it no longer, Bianchi drugged the woman's drink, threw her into the airplane, and flew her to his hunting camp in the woods. He indulged in his sexual fantasies before shooting her in the head and burying the woman in a shallow grave.

Bianchi knew that his bosses would disapprove of his little pastime, so he was careful to leave no evidence. Besides, he was married with five kids, not to mention a mistress and his pick of strippers. He possessed a raging libido and regularly partook of these goodies, but straight sex had long ago become boring. His fantasies were filled with images of helpless women. He constantly imagined one kneeling before him, begging for mercy, offering to do anything to stay alive. He loved the moment of truth and savored the pathetic look in their eyes. And pulling the trigger provided a climax more intense than the sex.

His brother had similar interests and soon joined him in the game, and together they perfected the operation. Bianchi would scout a suitable candidate, always a stripper or escort. Someone young, sexy, and naïve, living alone or in circumstances where their disappearance would go unnoticed. They kept the process simple. Select the victim, isolate and drug her, then fly her to their little camp. Enjoy a weekend of fun and bury the evidence. It was a perfect arrangement.

Until some asshole stumbled onto their camp and fucked it all up.

Everything had gone to shit in twenty-four hours. When he left camp, Tommy had things under control. They had broken the woman like a wild pony. Beaten and shocked into submission, she was eager to do anything to avoid the cattle prod. That included pleasing them in any manner they desired, and she'd been begging for it when Tony Bianchi left the camp. Tommy had a big day planned for her while his brother made a quick run to Seattle.

Bianchi returned the next morning to find a disaster. Tommy laid out on the ground, unconscious, with ugly burns covering his body. The woman disappeared. Bianchi searched the woods for her, cursing every step of the way and intent on putting a slug in her head. Finding no sign of her, he hurried back to Tommy.

His brother was a mess. A chunk missing from his skull, and his elbow and knee shattered. Bianchi loaded Tommy into the plane and flew back to Seattle, where they rushed Tommy into a surgical suite.

Doctors emerged hours later, shaking their heads. The trauma to his skull was severe. If Tommy survived, he would face years of rehab. The knee and elbow needed major reconstructive surgery and doctors warned they would never be fully functional. He couldn't shake his last image of Tommy. His brother's head wrapped like a mummy, tubes running out of every orifice and surgical wraps encasing his knee and elbow.

Bianchi felt the heat rise to his face at the thought of somebody sneaking up on his little brother and bashing in his head, then taking the time to shatter his arm and leg. There was no way the bitch had inflicted all that damage by herself. That asshole down there had brained Tommy, and Bianchi intended to inflict the most agonizing retribution on them both.

He glanced at the other man in the airplane.

His bosses in Jalisco had assigned Roca to him a year earlier. Roca had simply shown up one day and instructed him to call Jalisco if he had questions. Beyond the fact that Roca sprinkled salt into his Tecate beer, carried a nine-millimeter pistol in the small of his back, and concealed a filet knife in his boot, Bianchi knew little about the man. Roca walked with a pronounced limp and had a jagged scar running across his cheek. Bianchi had heard rumors that Roca was a respected cartel assassin, a brutal *Sicario* who fought on the front lines and had taken a bullet for the team.

Word was that Roca was sent to Seattle to recuperate and take a break from the drug wars.

Roca rarely spoke or questioned orders. Point him at a problem, and it went away. Roca hadn't said ten words since climbing into the airplane, stoically spending the hours staring through the binoculars. Bianchi welcomed the silence. He passed the time imagining the torture he would inflict on the two on the ground.

Vengeance wasn't Bianchi's sole motivation for wanting to take out the pair. He owned a string of bars and strip clubs in Seattle and also ran a busy escort service. These were lucrative and interesting operations, but they didn't represent his true profession. Bianchi used his bars and strip clubs to launder the millions generated by the Jalisco cartel. If the bitch made it out of these woods, she could cause trouble and disrupt business. That might prove fatal, and Bianchi wasn't about to let it happen.

Roca touched his shoulder and brought Bianchi out of his reverie. The Mexican jerked his head towards the back seat, where he had stowed an automatic rifle with a scope. "I can take care of them from here," he said.

Bianchi shook his head. "I want to handle it myself."

Roca shrugged and returned to the binoculars.

"See any problem?"

Roca shook his head. "I need a crew and a chopper. Won't take long. Maybe a day to set things up."

Bianchi swung the aircraft around and set the Cessna on a course back to Seattle. He glanced into the darkness and wished the pair down below a peaceful night. Soon enough, Hell's fury would descend on them.

CHAPTER THIRTY-TWO

Sarah was officially wealthy.

With a bang of his gavel, the Superior Court judge declared Evan Winslow deceased and directed the county medical examiner to issue a death certificate immediately. Sarah presented the document to her insurance agent, and the man handed over a certified check for a half-million dollars.

Brad Nixon proved to be an efficient and helpful attorney. At a lunch meeting the following week, he handed her another check, this one for two hundred thousand dollars. Nixon had undertaken a lengthy background investigation and discovered Evan purchased travel insurance before boarding the flight. Sarah was listed as the beneficiary. Nixon obtained the paperwork, filed the necessary documents and argued with adjusters, and came away with a full-figure settlement.

The attorney's work wasn't done. Nixon had another idea in mind, one with the potential for a more lucrative outcome. He suggested they file a lawsuit against Air

Pacific Airlines, as he considered the company liable for the tragedy. They discussed it at length, and Sarah gave him the go-ahead. Nixon suggested they demand ten million dollars and was confident the company would settle for half that amount.

Her bank account now held nearly three-quarters of a million dollars. The money was tax-free, and Nixon was confident she would receive millions more when the Air Pacific lawsuit was settled. Sarah would never again fret over a bill.

She was moving on in other ways.

She finally accepted the hard truth that Evan was not coming home. Flickering hopes for a miracle dashed by the passage of time, she had no desire to resurrect them. Sarah had worked through painful stages of denial, guilt, and anger She would never relinquish the regret filling her heart, but she had stopped tormenting herself with self-blame. She was determined to move on and began taking on difficult tasks of adjusting to a life alone. She spent a tough weekend packing his clothes into boxes. She donated it all to charity and bawled like a child when the truck drove away. She removed Evan's name from credit cards and checkbooks.

Some things she couldn't bear to let go. She left his study untouched and refused to put away treasured mementos or pictures on his walls. His golf clubs still sat in the corner of the garage. A bicycle gathered dust in another.

One evening she read his unfinished manuscript of Jeremy's Journey and realized he hadn't finished the story. A final chapter was needed. She tried to imagine an appropriate ending, and the spark of an idea entered her head. She poured herself a glass of wine and began writing the last chapter.

One huge and unfinished task loomed.

Sarah had a critical decision to make, one she'd been putting off for months and couldn't bear to make alone. She needed help, and she wanted it to come from someone in Evan's family. His parents had died years ago. His two older brothers had traveled to Arizona after Evan's disappearance. They were nice men, but the visit was awkward. Unsophisticated and uneducated, they seemed out of place in the city and uncomfortable with her grief. They didn't seem to know what to say or how to console her. After a few days they returned to West Virginia. She couldn't imagine calling them.

She thought of Evan's younger brother, Lucas. Sarah had never met him. She vaguely remembered that Lucas had gone to Berkeley and moved to Europe a decade ago. She decided to reach out to Lucas.

She hoped he might help her make the most difficult decision of her life.

CHAPTER THIRTY-THREE

"I don't believe it," Evan muttered.

He gazed at the documents scattered across the table, and a blast of adrenaline rattled through his body, setting his heart to thumping like a bass drum. The surge of juice revved up his system and got his hands trembling. He'd never felt such a rush. Thoughts of home momentarily vanished. He took a huge breath and willed himself to calm down.

Wanting to be certain, he again went through evidence Andrea had discovered. He unfolded and studied the topographical map. He scribbled a few notes, then closed his eyes and searched for holes in his theory. He went carefully over the evidence yet again, following a stream of logic that led him to the same inescapable conclusion each time. Finally, he convinced himself he was right.

Something monumental had happened out here. He had figured it out.

He ran to find Andrea.

She was sprawled on the grass, contemplating

a cloud bank and playing with her bunnies. She'd fashioned a roach clip from a bobby pin and was puffing on the remnant of a joint. She sat up and grinned at his wired-up appearance.

"You look like you just snorted a line of meth," she said.

"I'm buzzed, all right," he said, "because I've solved our mystery."

"Awesome," she said. "Tell me already."

"This was the hiding place of the world's most notorious hijacker."

"And that would be?"

"D. B. Cooper."

"Okay," she said slowly. "Never heard of him."

He was incredulous. "You don't recognize the name? D. B. Cooper's an urban legend. Back in the seventies….."

"Long before my time," she interrupted. "I'm a child of the nineties."

"Got it," he said. "Anyway, back in the seventies, a man using the name Dan Cooper hijacked a plane. Up here in the Northwest. The media mistakenly called him D. B. Cooper, and the name stuck."

"And you think this was his hideout?"

"I don't think it. I know it."

She shrugged and took a last hit from the roach flipping off the cherry and shaking the remnants of the weed into a baggie. "That's pretty cool, I guess.

You found some crook's hideout. What's got you so pumped?"

"I'm wired because D. B. Cooper was no ordinary criminal. He's a certified legend. This guy perpetrated the only unsolved commercial airplane hijacking in history. He was never caught. Never identified. He's risen to mythical status. Tons of books have been written about him. Television movies. Every few years, some network does a documentary."

"Okay, you have my attention." Andrea leaned forward, her face alive with intensity. "Tell me the whole story."

He unfolded a page of handwritten notes and ran his eyes down it. "Keep in mind this happened in the seventies," he said. "What I know comes from TV shows and documentaries. I've scribbled down what I remember. The stuff you found in the cabin filled in some blanks. The rest is guesswork."

He told her the story of D. B. Cooper.

In November of 1971, a man boarded a late-night commercial flight originating in Portland. He wore a business suit and dress shoes. Carried a briefcase. Sat in coach. Had a drink. Once the plane was airborne, he handed the stewardess a note. Claimed to have a bomb and demanded a ransom. He forced the pilot to land in Seattle. He released the passengers but held the crew hostage. Demanded money and parachutes. After they met his demands, Cooper ordered the plane back into the air. He instructed the pilot to fly a specific route, and he bailed out somewhere in southern Washington. He was never seen again.

"Got to admire the dude," she said. "Had the balls to hijack an airplane, collect ransom, and then jump out. You think he built this place as a hideout?"

"I have the evidence to prove it."

"And that's the money he stole?" She tilted her head towards the knapsack.

He nodded.

"I definitely need another number." She pulled out a baggie and rolled a joint. After taking a long pull, she said, "Okay, counselor, let's see your evidence."

He rummaged through the yellow envelope and handed her a blue and white rectangular booklet. "This is a Northwest Orient timetable published in 1971. It's the way they booked flights back then. You find the one you want in this book, then call and make a reservation. Cooper hijacked a Northwest flight in November of 1971."

He waited while she examined it, then handed her something else. "Now take a look at this. It's a schematic for a Boeing 707. That's the plane he hijacked."

She spent a while studying the document. "Could somebody jump out of a passenger plane without killing themselves?"

"It's possible with this particular aircraft," he said. "The hatch was located to the rear of the engines.

Theoretically, someone could bail out without being incinerated. That's exactly what Cooper did." He pulled another piece of paper from the folder and held it up. "This is the clincher."

Andrea appeared perplexed as she stared at it. "Bunch of lines above a map of the United States. Tell me what I'm looking at here."

"An FAA route map. Pilots used them to navigate in those days. One of those lines represents the route a passenger plane would follow to fly from Seattle to Reno. See the spot circled on it?"

She nodded.

"That has to be the spot where Cooper bailed out. I'm pretty sure it's in the vicinity of where we're sitting right now."

She looked at the knapsack. "How much did they pay him?"

"Two hundred thousand dollars," he said.

"So what happened to the other six thousand?"

"Maybe he'll tell us," he said. "If we run across him."

"I assume there are no finders-keepers?"

He shook his head. "It belongs to some bank. Or the government. If this is the ransom money, it was obtained in the commission of a federal crime. We turn it in, they'll seize it as evidence."

"Easy come, easy go," she said. She transferred the roach to the bobby pin before continuing. "I'm with you so far. But a few things about your scenario make no sense. You say he pulled this off in a business suit and dress shoes. Bailed out at night. In November. If he was such a criminal genius, why wasn't he dressed for cold weather? Why not pull off the job in the summer?"

"I'm betting he had his reasons," he said. "But everything else about this deal fits. There's no other explanation for what we've found here. Let's say our cabin builder's on trial, and we're the jury. He's charged with being the notorious hijacker D. B. Cooper. Would you vote to convict him?"

"Run the evidence by me again."

"We got the airline's timetable for the month and year of the hijacked flight. We got the schematic of the airplane he hijacked. And we have the route map showing he bailed out somewhere around here."

"Not to mention nearly two hundred thousand dollars lying around in an old cabin," she said.

"What's your verdict?"

"Friggin' guilty as hell," she declared, slamming down an invisible gavel. "Unanimous verdict." She lifted a bunny from its pen and set it on her lap. "But all we've discovered is this guy's hideout, and maybe the ransom money. We haven't solved the big mysteries. The ones that made D. B. Cooper a legend. Who the hell was he? And what happened to him?"

"We may never figure out that part," he said. "But I found one more interesting thing. It might lead us somewhere." He rummaged through the yellow envelope and held up a hand-drawn sketch.

"This is the plan for the cabin. Dimensions and measurements. It's got an interesting feature."

She squinted and stared at the drawing, then shrugged. "Like what?"

"See these dashed lines drawn underneath the floor? They outline an area beneath the floorboards. According to this diagram, there's a sizeable space under there."

"Ever more intrigue," she said. "Let's go see."

Inside the cabin, Evan studied the diagram and led her to a spot near the wall.

"According to the drawing," she said, looking over his shoulder, "we're standing on top of it."

He knelt and ran his hand over the rough boards. "This part of the flooring must give way or hinge."

She was staring at a spot where the floor and wall met. "This piece looks different."

A section of flooring abutted the wall. Unlike the rest of the room, its boards were of uniform length. Evan stuck his fingers in the crack between flooring and wall. He tugged upwards, and the hatch swung open.

"The hatch is rigged so you can close it with the wire from below." He flipped on the flashlight and shined it into the hole, and then he dropped through the opening.

Andrea stayed topside, peering into the crawlspace. "Anything interesting?"

"Just a hole in the ground," he said. "A blanket and a couple of dried out jugs. Cans of food. Some candles." He crawled out of the hole and replaced the hatch.

"Cooper thought of everything," she murmured. "Even built a hiding place inside his hiding place."

"Too bad he didn't leave clues down there about what happened to him."

"You got any theories?"

"My guess," he said, "is that he's still out here somewhere."

CHAPTER THIRTY-FOUR

Andrea plucked a wildflower and held it to her nose, enjoying its fragrant scent. Feeling as close to happy as she had managed in a long time. She had banished the horror to a dark corner of her mind. She envisioned it locked in an imaginary box. Anesthetized by the serenity of the forest and the magic of cannabis. She loved weed. It pushed away the damage inflicted by Tony Bianchi and calmed her in ways she couldn't describe. She imagined the drug as glittering pixie dust that allowed her to fly away from the shadows that haunted her.

She spotted a rainbow of colorful flowers growing along a dry creek bed. Something embedded in the ground caught her eye, and she noticed a disturbance in the dirt. She knelt and traced the outlines and decided they were boot prints.

Then she stepped on a bony arm.

She jumped back and shrieked. Embedded in long-dried mud were a skull and partially exposed torso. Bleached white and desiccated by decades of weather.

The bones covered by a ragged shirt and shredded jeans. A faded Mariner's cap alongside the skull. She shouted for Evan, and he came jogging up the creek bed, rifle across his shoulder.

"D. B. Cooper, I presume?"

"Who else?"

He returned to the cabin and fetched a shovel and hatchet. They cleared away the dirt, excavating the body with the care of an archaeological dig. A morning of hard work exposed the complete skeleton. Evan cut away the remains of the shirt.

"Look at his back." He pointed to the skeletal spine. "At least two major fractures. Could be more. There's a big crack on his skull."

"His right leg's shattered in a couple of places," she said. "Ribs are smashed."

Evan looked back at the cabin. It lay a quarter-mile distant. He turned to look up the stream bed, then he scratched his head. "Why leave the cabin in this condition? How did he make it this far? I'm amazed he could move at all."

"He won't be telling us anytime soon, that's for sure," Andrea said. "Let me show you something else." She led him down the creek bed, retracing the ancient footprints. She stopped and pointed. "What do you make of this?"

Animal tracks ran in tandem with those Cooper.

"Christ," he said. "Those are huge. Probably grizzly."

"A bear was following him?" she said.

He pulled away overgrown weeds and ran a hand over the tracks. "This is interesting."

"What's interesting?"

"Doesn't look like the bear was following him. The other way around. Cooper's footprints are on top – see how they displace the bear's? The grizzly went up the creek first, and he was following it."

"Why would anyone follow a bear?"

"I doubt he was hunting the thing, in his condition. Far as I can tell, he wasn't carrying a weapon."

"I'm wondering if he went a little crazy. Or if the cracked skull addled his brain. Why would he go after a grizzly bear? What the hell was he doing?"

Evan shrugged.

They used the shovel and hatchet to dig a final resting place for D. B. Cooper. They returned to the cabin and prepared to go home.

<hr />

Andrea spent her last evening working in the garden. He caught a trout from the pond, and they ate in silence at the rickety table. He was busy organizing his backpack when Andrea dropped the knapsack at his feet.

"What about this?"

"We take it with us and turn it in," he said, "along

with the evidence. If it's unclaimed, there's a chance we keep the money. That's unlikely. What we learned about D. B. Cooper is our bonanza. The world will go crazy that we found actual evidence. Every journalist and news magazine in the world will want to talk to us. Might even be a reward floating around. Or a book deal."

"I don't care about the money," she said, poking savagely at the fire. "And I definitely don't want to be famous."

"Okay," he said, raising his hands in surrender. "You asked."

"Yeah, I did," she said. "Sorry to unload on you."

"You okay?"

"Just not ready to go home."

"We have to go," he said. "It's time."

"Yeah," she said. "I know."

They talked until the fire died out and fell asleep under a full moon. Deep in the night, something awoke him. A million fireflies illuminated the meadow. Their fluorescent glow shone on the field like a psychedelic strobe.

Andrea danced among them, languidly waltzing with arms and face thrust skyward and moving in tempo to a tune only she could hear. It was a surreal sight, and he watched in awe. He was certain he would never experience anything as enchanting as watching this woman dance in the moonlight. She executed a graceful pirouette and danced towards him, extending her arms and pulling him to his feet.

They held one another beneath the full moon. He caught her rhythms, and they moved so naturally he had the feeling they had danced this way forever. The moon cast her face in a glow as she swirled around him. He made no effort to push away the emotions churning in his chest and allowed the sweetness of love to fill his heart. At that moment, he knew there was magic in the world. They danced and laughed until his head spun, then they walked hand in hand back to the fire.

A bright sunrise awoke them.

They exchanged sheepish smiles and prepared to break camp. He studied the topo map. Andrea stuffed necessary items into a duffel.

Both turned eyes to the sky when they heard concussive sounds.

A helicopter buzzed low over their heads.

"It's Bianchi," she said. "He found us."

CHAPTER THIRTY-FIVE

The chopper roared in low and hovered over the stump-filled clearing, rotors throwing dust in the air as Roca and his crew dropped to the ground. A three-man team, young, fit and lethal. All wore paramilitary camouflage and carried assault rifles. Overkill for this job, but Roca wanted no mistakes.

The cabin lay a hundred yards distant. He jerked his head towards it, and they spread into formation behind him and began carefully moving forward. The chopper rose into the air, and the pilot started circling in a wide arc. Roca could see Bianchi leaning out the window with binoculars held to his eyes.

Roca led his crew through rows of fruit trees and past a neatly tended garden, halting them with a raised fist before proceeding cautiously across the little meadow. He ran his eyes across the little cabin, confident the place would be empty. Their approach hadn't exactly been secretive, and the chopper noise would have flushed the pair like rabbits. Roca figured his quarry was running headlong through the forest, wide-eyed with panic and scrambling for a place to hide. They wouldn't get far. His team would quickly run them to ground if Bianchi didn't spot them from the air.

First he needed to clear the cabin.

He knelt beside the fire pit and extended a hand, feeling the warmth from a recent fire and noticing the remnants of a meal. His team moved closer and encircled the cabin. He jerked his head towards it, and a man crept to the window hole and looked inside before turning and shaking his head. Roca belly-crawled to the open door and cocked an ear, then stepped into the cabin and did a quick visual sweep. As he expected, it was deserted.

He returned to the meadow and stood over a little pen, gazing pensively at the pair of rabbits. Then he jogged back into the cabin and did a more careful walkthrough. There was nowhere to hide in the tiny room. Roca went back outside, gathered his team, and they pressed into the forest.

Evan and Andrea lay in the hole beneath the cabin's floorboards.

The floor creaked and groaned as heavy footsteps echoed overhead. He held Andrea's trembling body in his arms, watching motes of dust that floated in slivers of light shining through the floor's cracks.

Despite their peril, his mind kept returning to last night's moonlight dance. The radiance of her face. The electric shock of her body pressed against his chest. The rise and fall of her breasts as she swirled across the meadow. He knew what she had been feeling. The freedom and joy provided by the simple act of dancing allowed her to forget for a moment the horror that now walked above them.

When the footsteps faded, he crawled to a thin shaft of light shining through a foundation crack. Four men stood in a circle outside the cabin. A muscular Hispanic man in camouflage spoke into his collar, and the helicopter's thumping grew faint. The man uttered a command in Spanish, then he strode into the forest, and the other men followed.

Evan returned to Andrea and pulled her close.

"They're gone," he whispered.

She burrowed into his arms and he felt her shuddering body and the wetness of her tears. "I won't go through it again," she cried. "I'll kill myself before Bianchi touches me."

"He'll never touch you," he promised.

CHAPTER THIRTY-SIX

Bianchi called off the search at dusk and ordered Roca's team to remain on the ground. The Mexican set up camp in the meadow while Bianchi flew off to Seattle. Overnight, the situation became more perilous. A call from Jalisco. Not from *el jefe* himself, but a lieutenant high enough in the pecking order to merit Bianchi's attention. The man spoke flawless English and minced no words. A disruption in operations had been noticed in Bianchi's area. A drop in distribution and cash flow, serious enough to merit a call and a question.

Is there a problem?

Hell yes, there's a problem, Bianchi thought, but he couldn't tell the man the truth. He couldn't confess that he was a sexual deviate and a serial killer who murdered innocent women for pleasure. That instead of laundering cash, he was wasting his time chasing down a woman with enough knowledge to cause major headaches for the cartel. That if she escaped the woods and started blabbing, Roca would surely be ordered to put a slug in his head.

So he lied.

He told the man that he'd discovered an informant in the organization, a low-level distributor seen talking to a DEA agent. The snitch had disappeared, but Roca was running him down and the problem would be resolved shortly. The lieutenant listened in stony silence, then curtly advised Bianchi to handle it and get distribution back to normal.

No threat was issued, but none was necessary.

That was yesterday, and Bianchi felt sweat dripping from his face as he recalled the conversation. He drummed stubby fingers on the console and stared at the empty forest. They had searched every square inch of a five-mile grid running west of the cabin. Roca was certain the pair would run straight for the coast, but a day of air and ground searches turned up squat. Roca had got it wrong. Bianchi decided to redirect the hunt, so he ordered the pilot to turn to the north, towards a long mountain range.

The chopper banked and swung around while Bianchi slid open a window and raised the binoculars to his eyes. The pilot was looking out the other window. They were about to run out of airspace when the pilot thumped his arm and gestured towards the ground.

Two people were running through a stand of aspen trees.

"Got you, bitch," Bianchi muttered.

The pilot marked the spot on his GPS, then he tilted the helicopter and sped off to pick up Roca's team. The sun was dropping in the sky when the pilot nudged Bianchi and tapped the fuel gauge. The big man swore in frustration, then he radioed Roca and advised him to settle in for another night.

The pilot banked to the west and headed back to Seattle.

⚬⊲◆⊳⚬

They dove for cover as the helicopter buzzed their heads. The craft briefly hovered overhead before it spun away, and they watched until the craft became a speck on the horizon. "They've gone to get the others," he said.

Andrea began running towards the foot of the mountain, and they kept a steady pace until darkness forced a halt. A fire was out of the question, so he used the flashlight to illuminate the backpack. He rummaged through it and found an unlabeled can that turned out to be peaches, and that was dinner.

Night fell. The moon bathed the woods in a buttery glow and cast the trees in shadow. They lay on their backs and stared at the moon's cratered surface, listening to the chirping of cicadas. Andrea rested near him, gazing into the sky.

"The bunnies," she said.

"We'll go back for them."

"No, we won't," she said. We're going to die tomorrow."

"Don't talk that way," he said. "Nobody's dying tomorrow."

"That chopper's coming back in the morning," she said in a low voice, "full of men with guns. They'll shoot us or turn us over to Bianchi, and he'll bury us out here. Either way, we're not leaving these woods alive." She reached over and touched his hand. "Sorry I got you into this mess."

"This isn't your fault," he said. "You tried to warn me about Bianchi, but I didn't listen. Now I get it. We'll be more careful from now on. When they come back tomorrow, we'll be long gone. There's a lot of places to hide out here. We'll stay in the trees and won't light fires. They'll never find us."

"You're still underestimating Bianchi," she said. "There's nobody like him in your world. He's nuts. He has unlimited resources, and he won't stop looking for me. I know what they did. I know where they buried the bodies. And he'll come for you, after what you did to his brother. He'll be back tomorrow, and the next day, and the one after that. He'll bring more people with guns. Airplanes. Dogs. Even if we get away from him and make it home, he'll eventually find us. And he'll kill us."

"That won't happen," he said in a patient voice. "He won't find us. We'll make it home and go to the authorities. We'll tell them about that camp. They'll arrest him, and he'll never bother you again."

"He'll always bother me," she said. She massaged her neck with a hand as she rummaged through the backpack and pulled out a baggie. "Interested?"

He nodded, so she rolled and lit a joint, took a long drag, and passed it over. Her face creased into a little smile as he raised the joint to his lips.

"You get home, you gonna tell 'em you're a stoner?"

He released the smoke and watched it curl into the sky. "It'll be our secret."

She rolled onto her back and stuck the backpack beneath her head, gazing up into the universe. He watched her as she stared into the night, looking at things he couldn't see and feeling things he couldn't know. Her face was soft in the starlight, and her features appeared fragile, like fine porcelain.

"You can get past what they did to you," he said softly.

"I don't think so."

He moved over to lay beside her and laid a hand on her arm. "People survive trauma," he said. "You can't see it right now, but one day you'll feel differently. I'll help you get through it, if you want."

She was quiet for a long time, then she said, "When I was a kid, my parents took me to the zoo. An old-school one where they kept the animals in these tiny cages in an old brick building with no ventilation or windows. They had every kind of animal in there, locked side-by-side in those little spaces. I remember standing in front of a cage and watching an old lion. He just laid in that tiny cage, with no energy or life, and I could see this horrible sadness in its eyes. That cage sucked everything out of him. His pride. His strength and energy. His will to live. I felt so sad, because I knew that lion would never be free. Even if they released him into the jungle, he would never again be a lion. It might look like one, but it would just be a poor, broken animal. I remember that I started crying and ran out of there."

"I get what you're saying," he said. "But there's a difference between you and that lion. If you think you're locked in a cage, remember that you have the key. You can unlock the door and free yourself. I've spent my life helping people overcome bad things, and I know something about healing. I promise that you won't always feel this way. You'll eventually want to get on with your life, and there's help out there, other trauma survivors who know what you're feeling and can help you get past it."

She took a hit off the joint and passed it over. "I appreciate the pep talk, doc," she said. "I'll give it some thought." She sat up and crossed her legs. "Change of subject. I want you to make me a promise."

"What would that be?"

"Let's split up in the morning. You go one direction and I'll go another. We'll meet up back in civilization."

He shook his head. "Better we stay together."

"It's logical, if you think about it," she said. "If we split up, we increase our chances of getting away. One person can hide easier than two, and they'll have to divide up to go after us. And don't forget I'm the one Bianchi wants. He knows nothing about you. He doesn't even know your name. You make it out of here and go home, and he'll never find you."

"Those are good points," he said. "But no, Andrea. We stay together."

"Please," she said. "Do this one thing for me. I got you into this mess in the first place. You saved my life more than once. Let me do something to repay you. I promise he won't catch me. I'll run fast and hide. We'll both get away. You can go home to Sarah and resume your life. I owe you that much."

"You don't owe me anything," he said. "Besides, you'd never make it home."

"I don't want to go home," she said.

He gave her a puzzled look. "What do you mean?"

"I want to stay here."

"In these woods?"

She nodded.

"That doesn't even make sense," he said. "You can't

survive out here. Even if I stayed with you, living in the wilderness takes skills we don't possess."

"D. B. Cooper did it."

"Look how he ended up," he said.

"Okay," she said, raising her hands in capitulation. "Bad example. But I still want us to split up."

"I know what you're trying to do," he said. "And I appreciate it. But we're not splitting up, and that's the end of it. We'll get moving early in the morning. We'll make it home and go straight to the cops. Bianchi will spend the rest of his life in prison and never bother you again. Okay?"

"Okay," she said.

CHAPTER THIRTY-SEVEN

Andrea was gone when he awoke.

Missing was her backpack and the knapsack full of cash. In their place, a folded piece of notebook paper was secured under a small rock. He uttered a curse as he stuffed the note in his pocket and peered into the woods. He called her name, but the concussive sounds of the helicopter washed away his voice. The craft dropped onto a clearing a hundred yards away, and a mass of men boiled out. He grabbed his pack and rifle and sprinted into the woods, dodging through trees and continuing to call her name.

Pursuers were closing fast as he unslung the rifle and fired off a volley of rounds, causing them to scatter and dive for cover. He continued his headlong flight, racing up a sloping hill and turning onto a ridgeline. Jumping behind a tree, he looked down the slope and spotted a pair of men scrambling up the trail behind him.

The men abruptly stopped their pursuit.

One put a finger to his ear and said something into his collar. The pair exchanged words, then spun and jogged back into the woods. The helicopter buzzed his location before banking and speeding away. He ran along the ridgeline, trying to keep the chopper in sight. The craft abruptly stopped and hovered above an open meadow.

Andrea ran out of the trees.

Passing beneath the chopper, she stopped at the meadows edge and reached into the knapsack. Bundles of cash went flying into the chopper's churning wash, and a mass of twenty-dollar bills swirled across the meadow. Andrea waved merrily at the occupants of the helicopter, then spun and ran back into the woods. A string of men carrying firearms emerged from the other side of the meadow. Spotting the tornado of money, they immediately forgot their quarry and began a frenzied cash grab.

The helicopter dropped onto the ground, and a heavyset man emerged. He awkwardly crabbed from beneath the chopper's rotors, pulling out a white handkerchief and mopping his shaven head.

Evan knew he was looking at Tony Bianchi.

He watched as Bianchi pulled a pistol from his belt and fired it into the air.

The presence of their boss seemed to bring his money-crazed henchmen to their senses. Bianchi barked out a command and jerked a thumb towards the woods. The men reluctantly stopped stuffing cash into their pockets and resumed their pursuit of Andrea.

Bianchi followed them towards the forest edge, moving in a clumsy sailor's lurch as he laboriously moved his corpulent body across the field.

Evan sighted down the rifle's scope, centering the crosshairs on Bianchi's head, then he exhaled slowly and pulled the trigger. The shot echoed across the meadow, causing the big man to flinch and duck. Foot soldiers emerged from the trees and ran to protect Bianchi, directing a barrage of gunfire in Evan's direction.

Ignoring the fusillade of bullets, he kept the rifle trained on Bianchi's wide body, centering the man's hefty chest in the crosshairs. As he pulled the trigger, another echoing discharge burst forth. A blossom of crimson erupted on Bianchi's dress shirt. The man clutched his chest and dropped to the ground.

Bianchi's men laid down covering fire while others dragged the man's body onto the helicopter. They clambered aboard and the chopper buzzed away at high speed. Evan ran back into the forest, shouting Andrea's name.

He couldn't imagine why she might still be hiding. She couldn't have run far and surely saw the helicopter fly away. He finally broke off the fruitless search at dusk and built a roaring fire in hopes of drawing her out of the woods. He pulled out her note and read it in the flickering firelight.

Evan.

You are the most decent man I have ever known. And the bravest. You risked your life to save me, and I will forever be grateful. I can't stay here any longer. Something's broken inside me, and it left a stain I can never wash away.

Thank you for everything. For letting me share your journey and allowing me to feel loved for a little while. Thank you for the cave, the cabin, and the fireflies. I'm sorry to leave this way. Please don't come after me. Go home to Sarah and enjoy your life. Think of me when you see fireflies.

We'll meet again someday. I promise.

Andrea.

He stared into the flames. *Where was she going? What was she planning to do?* It had to be the cabin. She loved that place. She wanted to rescue her bunnies. She couldn't be going anywhere else.

He awoke at dawn and hefted the backpack, studying the horizon until he found the snow-capped peak to the north and jagged volcanic fissure to the south. Hiking westward, by early afternoon he arrived at a point roughly between the two peaks. He turned towards the south, now walking in the direction of the fissure. When night fell, he camped in the trees and didn't bother to eat. He drank from a stream and crawled into the bag, and at first light he was back on the trail to the cabin.

He approached quietly and remained in the shadows of trees, studying the place through binoculars. He remained in hiding for an hour, scanning the meadow and trees. Vigilant for the sound of a helicopter. Finally, he crossed the field and stepped into the cabin.

He shined a light into the crawl space beneath the floorboards, then went into the meadow and sat at the rickety table, noticing freshly cut flowers in the antique Coke bottle. Garden greens in a bowl. He walked to the pen beside the cabin and saw the bunnies sleeping on the ragged blanket, a pile of fresh clippings beside them.

Andrea had been here.

He built a fire and sipped whiskey from the bottle. He reread the note, then he threw it in the fire. Fireflies gathered in the meadow and bathed the night in emerald strobe, and for a moment he thought he saw her dancing in the flickering lights. He blinked, and the image was gone.

He lay back and stared at the stars, thinking about Andrea. And Sarah. He couldn't remember his wife's face or smile. He tried to summon his feelings for her. He knew that he loved Sarah, but tonight he couldn't feel it. His thoughts kept pulling him back to Andrea. A three-day hike, and he would be home to Sarah. But Andrea was alone in the wilderness. She wouldn't survive out here without him. He poked at the fire until fireflies extinguished their glow. He dozed off, but a thought jolted him awake.

The cave.

Andrea's hideout. Less than a day's hike from the cabin. A place she loved nearly as much as the cabin. If not here, she would be there. At first light, he lifted the bunnies out of their pen and carried them to the garden, where he released them. They ran down a furrow and disappeared into the greenery.

He hiked steadily throughout the day. The sun was dropping behind the horizon when he arrived at the waterfall. He stared into the pond, watching spray rise into the air. For an instant, he saw her floating above it, framed by a rainbow and appearing ghostly and opaque. He walked behind the waterfall and into the cave. He gazed at the stick drawings and ran a finger over the plus sign she'd drawn to connect them.

Beneath the stick figures, a fresh picture - a heart drawn in mud and pierced by an arrow. On the ground, a baggie containing four rolled joints. Flowers at the cabin, and now a stash of marijuana. Why was she visiting the places she loved and leaving him gifts? He stared at the mud heart and wondered if she might be planning something extreme.

For two days, he sat atop a knoll and watched the woods. At night, he smoked weed and sorted through options. Where else might he search for her? How long to look? When to set out for home? Finally, he scratched a message on the wall, telling her he would wait a week at the cabin.

Then he would go home.

He waited a restless week before spreading out the old map. He traced a finger along the pencil-drawn route. He estimated forty miles to the winding river and another twenty miles to arrive at the dirt road. Five miles further along, marked on the map with a little star, was a small logging town.

He took a final look at the cabin, and then he began his march for home. He carried no food or provisions. He stopped at streams for water, and one morning he shot a small antelope. He roasted and consumed its flank, then stowed what was left in his backpack. He heard the river before he saw it, and that night slept beside the rushing waters. He resumed his homeward trek, lost in his thoughts until a sound caused him to glance over his shoulder.

A grizzly shuffled twenty yards behind him. He recognized the distinctive white patch on its rump and knew this was his bear. The animal stopped to sniff the ground and tear at something with its massive claws. He felt a sense of comfort at the presence of the bear. It had been with him from the beginning, and it seemed appropriate that it accompany him to the end.

Late in the day, he climbed a small hill to gain his bearings. He raised the binoculars and studied the landscape, spotting a forested valley in the distance. Beyond it lay a checkerboard pattern of farmland and a winding dirt road.

CHAPTER THIRTY-EIGHT

Sarah scanned the stream of deplaning passengers.

All pulling roller bags. Eyes glued to electronic devices. She easily picked out Lucas when he walked through security. He bore a strong resemblance to his older brother. The same dark brows and chiseled features as Evan. His hair was long and graying beneath a battered fedora, and a well-used backpack hung across his shoulder.

He had the appearance of a new age hippie or itinerant musician.

Sarah was meeting Lucas for the first time and knew little about him. Highly educated. An inveterate traveler who had spent most of his life abroad.

And the family's black sheep.

She waved, and he pushed through the crowd towards her.

Lucas greeted her warmly as they exchanged hugs and pleasantries. His face was relaxed and smiling, his voice deep and resonant, and an aura of calm surrounded him. When they spoke, he gazed earnestly into her eyes, and Sarah felt an immediate connection. She asked about his trip, and Lucas described the six-hour flight from Frankfurt into New York as boring, followed by an equally tedious nonstop to Phoenix. He expressed interest in a drink, so they detoured into an airport bar.

"So, you're Evan's gypsy brother," she said.

He chuckled. "It's true I've done my share of traveling. I left home a year after Evan and never went back."

"You've never returned home in all these years?"

"Long story," he said. "One for another day."

She nodded and changed the subject. "You were close, weren't you?"

"As close as brothers can be."

"He told me some things about your childhood," she said. "Sounds like it wasn't the easiest."

"We were dirt poor," Lucas said. "Hillbillies in the truest sense. Our parents didn't finish grammar school and married as teenagers. Daddy went into the coal mines at sixteen and stayed in them for thirty years, making starvation wages. We shot game for the dinner table and ate what we grew from the garden. Every piece of clothing I had was a hand-me-down from Evan, and those were passed down to him from the two oldest."

"I've met your brothers," she said.

"I haven't seen them in years," Lucas said. "I

remember them as pure country. All about pickup trucks. Bluegrass music and fishing. Neither of them graduated high school. They went straight into the mines as teenagers, and I'm sure they're still digging coal. Then Evan comes along and breaks the mold. A top student. Played sports and stayed out of trouble. Coal mining was the last thing he wanted. He would spend hours looking at maps, marking off the places he planned to see. As soon as he graduated high school, he left those hills and went off to pursue his dream."

"And you followed in his footsteps?"

Lucas nodded. "I left home the summer after high school. He'd gone west, so I headed in the same direction. I stopped here in Arizona but kept moving and eventually ended up in California. Hustled my way through college, just like Evan. He got his doctorate, so I had to have one. Somehow got into Berkeley. Evan studied psychology, so I chose philosophy. After graduation, I took a year off. Wanted to see the world. Europe seemed like a perfect place to start."

"Sounds like a grand adventure."

"The time of my life. I flew into Frankfurt with a hundred dollars in my pocket. I waited tables, taught skiing, even freelanced a couple of pieces for a travel magazine. On a whim, I applied for a position in the philosophy department at the University of Heidelberg. I had a brand-new doctorate and spoke decent German, so they offered me a visiting professor position. Spent a couple of years at Cambridge. Even did a year at Oxford."

"Have doctorate, will travel," she quipped.

"The nomadic moralist," he said, smiling.

"A long way from the creeks and hollers of West Virginia," Sarah said, raising her drink in salute.

"I owe it all to my big brother."

"I'm glad you're here," she said. "The next part won't be easy."

"I've spent the past week trying to prepare for it."

While driving through late afternoon traffic, Sarah did her best to explain what he was about to experience. She parked in the visitor's lot of a modern glass building and waved at the receptionist as they walked onto the elevator. She led him through a warren of corridors until they arrived at the room.

She stopped at the door and turned to Lucas, putting a hand on his arm. "You won't recognize him," she said.

He nodded, and they walked into the hospital room.

A man lay on the bed.

His body rail-thin, he appeared a hundred years old. His face was aged and wizened. Machines surrounded the bed, wires and tubes ran into his body. A saline drip provided fluids, a narrow tube was taped to a nostril, and a larger blue line ran from a mechanical ventilator into his mouth. The ventilator hissed and caused his chest to rise and fall rhythmically. A halo brace immobilized his head. His left arm was encased in a cast from elbow to wrist.

Sarah watched as Lucas walked to the bed. His face filled with compassion as he gently took the man's hand.

"Hello, brother," he said.

CHAPTER THIRTY-NINE

Lucas's face paled. He shuddered and began to tremble as he stared at his brother's devastated body. Sarah moved close and placed a hand on his shoulder. "I know it's a shock to see him this way," she said.

"You told me what to expect," he said, his voice shaky with emotion. "But I can't believe it. How long has he been like this?"

"Almost two years."

"You said he was in an airplane crash," he said. "Can you tell me what happened?"

"He was flying home from Seattle when his plane disappeared from radar. It was missing two weeks before they found the wreckage. Seventeen passengers onboard. Everyone died, except Evan."

Lucas continued gazing at Evan's shattered body. "I can't imagine how he lived through the crash."

"An engine malfunction caused the airplane to break apart in midair," she said. "The experts think he fell almost five miles, and they speculated that some tree branches broke his fall. He landed about a quarter-mile from where they found the wreckage. Somehow, he survived. When the search team arrived, things were chaotic. They did a body count and realized one was missing. It took another two days before they found him. He was a couple of miles from the crash site. Unconscious. Had a broken back and multiple leg fractures."

"Why did it take so long to find him?"

"Government incompetence," she said, "If they'd found him sooner, who knows? He might have recovered."

She shook her head in frustration. "They didn't put any effort into looking for him. At first, the assholes even refused to admit the plane had crashed. They insisted it was just an electronic glitch, and everything was fine. Nothing to worry about. They finally brought in a search and rescue team but couldn't locate the plane and called it off after a week. I begged them to keep looking. Even flew to Seattle, but it didn't matter. They had other priorities and stopped looking for him. Just left him out there to die."

"Then who found him?"

"An air traffic controller in Seattle. He was on duty the night the plane left Seattle. For some reason, he felt responsible for the plane's disappearance and became obsessed with finding it. He kept looking after everybody else gave up. He sorted through thousands of satellite pictures and eventually spotted the wreckage. He sounded the alarm, and a rescue team went back out there. God only knows how Evan survived. Everyone called it a miracle."

"I'm not so sure," Lucas said.

"Sometimes I wish he'd died with the rest of them."

Her lip trembled as she stared at the machines surrounding her husband's body. "They're keeping him alive with damned machines. Feeding him through tubes. He can't even breathe on his own. Nobody should go through what he's experienced. He's lain in this bed for two years, enduring the most horrible pain. It's so unfair. There's so much more he would've done with his life."

"So much more *we* could've done."

Lucas laid a consoling hand atop hers and waited until her tears passed. "You said he struck the ground about a quarter-mile from where the plane went down? But they found him somewhere else?"

"He somehow dragged himself over to the wreckage. He built some fires. Salvaged things from luggage. Fed himself. Even tended to the bodies of the other passengers. I can't imagine how he managed any of it. The pain must have been excruciating. The rescuers think he stayed at the crash site about a week."

"Where did they finally find him?"

"A couple of miles to the west."

She could see Lucas trying to put it together in his mind. "Let me make sure I understand," he said. "He fell from an airplane, miraculously survived the impact, and then crawled to the crash site. Stayed there a week, waiting for rescue. When nobody showed up, he decided to make his way home. Is that what you're thinking?"

"That's exactly what I think," she said. "He had a backpack filled with survival gear. He was heading west. But he didn't get far. Like I said, his back and legs were broken. It's a miracle he could even move. He was comatose and barely alive when they found him. They airlifted him to Seattle, and when he was stable they transferred him here. He's been in this bed for the past two years."

"He probably knew making it home was impossible," Lucas said, "but that wouldn't stop him. He always was stubborn as a country mule."

"Really? Even as a kid?"

"Let me tell a story about Evan. He took an Army ROTC class in high school. He was interested in the military. They gave him a uniform and a toy rifle, and every afternoon they marched behind the school. An old retired Army sergeant ran the class. I guess Evan was having trouble with a drill, so the sarge told him to stay out there and work on it. The sergeant went home and forgot about Evan. It got dark and he hadn't come home, so my daddy sent me to look for him. I found him at midnight, still marching around that field. He wouldn't stop until the sarge came back and relieved him."

"Doesn't surprise me," she said. "It's the story of his life."

Lucas was examining his brother's face, which was frozen into a grimace. His mouth wide open, and his head tilted back. His eyes rolled upwards, staring at nothing. His chest continued to move up and down in rhythm with the hiss of the ventilator.

"What are you thinking about?" Sarah said.

Lucas shrugged. "Childhood stuff. The two of us running through the hills. Chasing one another across the playground. Trying to hold onto the good memories. I don't want to remember him this way."

"He'll never again be that person," she said. "It took me a year to accept it. Another year to start moving on with life."

"Has he ever regained consciousness?"

"Sometimes, he seemed close. We did everything imaginable to bring him out of it. The doctors ran all their tests and said his brain was still active and capable of processing information. So I tried to stimulate his mind in any way possible. It became my mission. I came here nearly every day. I read to him. Kept him up on world events. Left the television running. Played his favorite music."

"Did he ever react?"

"I don't know," she said. "Maybe. He would twitch or jerk his legs. I think he knew when I was in the room. I'd kiss him on the cheek or say his name, and sometimes I was sure I felt him respond."

Lucas noticed the cast encasing his brother's left arm and reached over to touch it. "That looks new."

"He fell out of bed a couple of months ago. He'd barely moved for nearly a year, then one morning he just tumbled over the side. Broke his arm and sustained another brain injury. His back was already messed up, and the fall ruined it. The surgeons did what they could. Implanted rods and pins in his spine and put him on pain killers. It was obvious that he was more comfortable after the surgery."

She moved to Evan's bedside and began rubbing a thick cream onto his skin. Lucas picked up the jar and examined it.

"Cannabidiol? Cannabis extract?"

She nodded and smiled. "To help with the pain. I've been using it on him for weeks."

"Wonder if he feels it," he said.

"I don't know," she said. "Can't hurt, right?"

As she rubbed the ointment onto her husband's unresponsive body, Sarah could see fatigue creep into Lucas' face. She ushered him from the hospital, insisting he stay in her guest room. Lucas put up no resistance and was quiet during the ride home.

She pulled a couple of steaks from the freezer and set out plates and silverware. She heard the shower running, and after a while Lucas emerged from the bedroom.

"I am reborn," he said with a smile. She accepted his offer to cook the steaks and led him to the grill on the patio.

Scanning the wine cabinet, she removed a Cabernet, then impulsively decided a Zinfandel better suited the menu. She uncorked and decanted the wine into a crystal carafe, watching Lucas grill the steaks. He turned in profile, and from that perspective he could have been Evan. It caused a familiar ache to rise, and she thought wistfully of days forever gone. She turned from the window and concentrated on putting together a salad.

They talked over dinner. Lucas wanted to know about his brother's life and career. His hobbies and interests. Their life together. Sarah's work. After dinner, they moved outside and opened another bottle of wine.

"I still can't believe that's my brother in the hospital bed."

"The person you saw today's no longer Evan," she said with a sad smile. "He left this world two years ago, and he's not coming back. It's taken me a long time to find peace with knowing I'll never again talk to him."

"Must have been hell," he said.

"I was as paralyzed as him for the first year. The depression was horrible, and I had these mood swings that made me do crazy things. I've gotten past most of it, and medication keeps me pretty much under control."

"I wish I'd known. Maybe I could have helped in some way."

"My fault, really," she said. "I should have contacted you. It crossed my mind, but I wasn't thinking clearly. I figured your brothers would let you know."

"They didn't make an effort," he said, "which doesn't surprise me."

"Evan never said much about the falling-out."

Lucas shrugged. "I was young and selfish, and I did something stupid. My senior year of high school, daddy became ill with black lung disease. I was itching to get out of the hills and didn't pay much attention to him. Momma begged me to stay home to help look after him. My brothers didn't want me to go. I didn't care. After graduation, I headed west. Daddy died the next year."

Lucas shrugged and raised his hands. "I skipped the funeral. I was a broke college kid, two thousand miles from home and no way to get there. That added to the rift. Then Momma died the next year, and nobody bothered to let me know. That was it for my family. My brothers pretty much disowned me, and I felt the same towards them. We haven't spoken since."

"Evan always spoke fondly of you."

"I think we just lost touch. I've been living in Europe and haven't been to the states in years. I was living a vagabond life, no roots, moving around all the time."

"I'm glad you're here now," she said. "I don't want to make this decision alone."

"I'm grateful you tracked me down. I want to help you."

She raised a finger as a thought entered her mind. "There's something I want to show you."

Sarah walked into the house and returned carrying a manuscript.

"He was writing this story," she said. "I thought you might want to read it."

"Jeremy's Journey," he said as he studied the cover page. "I never knew he was a writer. What's it about?"

"It's a kid's book. A boy named Jeremy's lost in the wilderness. He and a playmate have adventures as they try to find their way home."

"Sounds like good bedtime reading," Lucas said. "I'm going to start tonight."

CHAPTER FORTY

Sarah rose early and walked through her garden. She searched among the blooms until finding the Charlotte, a small flower with a beautiful yellow hue and a pleasing fragrance. She studied the plant before snipping a perfect blossom and carrying it to the patio.

She would take it to the hospital and place it in a small crystal vase by Evan's bed. She preferred fragrant blooms such as the Charlotte, believing he might enjoy its scent. Lucas emerged from the kitchen and handed her a steaming cup of coffee. They sat on the patio and talked about the coming day.

The first order of business was a return visit to the hospital, where she introduced Lucas to the medical team. They were led into a wood-paneled conference room, where the doctors reviewed Evan's case. The medical experts laid before them an array of reports and test results. Brain stem reflex measures. EEG findings. Pupillary reflex tests. Each doctor took a turn presenting their grim findings. Cranial blood flow patterns. The persistent minimal brain activity represented by a continuous flat line interrupted only by an occasional random spike. They spoke at length about Evan's persistent non-responsiveness to pain stimulation.

The proof was overwhelming.

The experts were unanimous in their conclusions.

Evan was brain-dead.

Afterward, in the hospital cafeteria, their coffee remained untouched as they sat in silence. Lucas put his head into his hands and began to tremble and cry. This started Sarah's tears flowing. She came around the table and sat beside him, putting an arm around his shoulder. They cried out their sadness and grief, mourning someone they loved and would never again know.

Lucas gathered himself, taking a couple of deep breaths and giving her a lopsided smile. "I'm okay now," he said.

"It's so awful," she said. "I'm so sorry."

"I'm the one who should apologize. Falling apart. Blubbering on your shoulder. I can't imagine what this ordeal's been like for you."

"I never stopped believing he'd wake up," she said. "I waited two years for a miracle that never came."

Lucas stared into his coffee. "I guess we should talk about the next step."

She nodded.

"You sure you're ready?"

"I'll never be ready," she said. "But it's not about me. It's about Evan. I know he's ready for it to end."

"You ever talk about it?"

"No. I mean, who anticipates your spouse in an irreversible coma? Or hashing out when to pull the plug? We focused on living. Building careers and planning for the future. Dealing with day-to-day problems. It was never a topic of conversation."

"You know him better than anyone," Lucas said. "What would he want?"

"Not this," she said.

"Any legal or ethical issues?"

"The doctors have been urging me for months to make the decision. You heard them this morning. There's no hope. Evan's in an irreversible coma. A judge declared him legally deceased months ago. I have the right to make the decision, and the hospital lawyers have signed off. The medical people are just waiting for my approval to discontinue life support."

"What's the process involve?"

"They'll take him off the ventilator and remove the feeding tube. They'll stop the medications that keep his vital organs functioning. They'll continue to hydrate his body. Give him medicine for pain."

"How long before…..?"

"Not long." Her voice tremored, and she took in gulps of air to calm herself. "He won't know what's happening. He won't feel anything. After a while, he'll just stop breathing. Then he'll be gone."

"God, this is tough," he said, running a hand through his hair. "We're sitting here drinking coffee and talking about letting my brother suffocate. I know it's time to let him go. But it's hard to imagine going through with it."

"It's been tearing me apart for months. Every day I come in here and see him this way. But I haven't been able to let him go. It's why I needed your help, Lucas."

She watched as tears again filled his eyes. "There's no other choice, is there?"

"No," she said. "It's time."

They stopped by his room, and Sarah placed the yellow rose in the crystal vase. She filled it with water and gave her husband a tender kiss.

The mortuary sprawled across acres of prime real estate at the periphery of Scottsdale. They pulled in front of ornate double gates that swung open at their approach. A winding cobblestone lane led them through grounds landscaped with desert plants, colorful flowers, and tall Saguaro cactus. The facility had the appearance of a small university with its clusters of buildings and campus-like feel.

They stood before a huge sign that provided

directions to administrative offices, a chapel, mausoleum, memorial park, and cemetery. Walking along a flagstone path, they stopped to gaze at the beautiful Mediterranean-style mausoleum built with Italian marble and accessed through a gated courtyard.

A compassionate funeral director loaded them onto a golf cart and took them on a tour of the grounds, pointing out particular features. Afterward, they sat before a large oak desk while the director walked them through a checklist of necessary actions. Every step involved multiple choices, every choice required a decision, and every decision carried a hefty price tag. They spent an hour leafing through a stack of thick catalogs and making sad choices. The size and scope of the service. Type and extent of flowers. The appropriate form of musical accompaniment. Who would speak at the eulogy. The preferred religious theme. Details of the processional to the internment site.

Even the issue of cremation was more complicated than Sarah had figured. The funeral director gently advised them of the alternatives for handling Evan's remains. A columbarium niche. Or the remains could be interred in the mausoleum. Another option was an urn buried in a garden located on the grounds, with a tree or shrub planted beside it. The director confided this was a popular alternative. A final option would be to scatter the ashes in a location of their choosing.

Sarah selected a large and ornate urn and decided it would be interred in a columbarium niche. Finally, they went through a small book filled with plaques, and Lucas helped her compose an inscription.

It was past dark when they returned home. Exhausted and despondent from the misery of the day, Sarah held up an expensive bourbon.

"Feel like getting drunk?"

"Definitely," he said.

She filled two crystal snifters, and they drank Evan's favorite whiskey. She lit one of his cigars and let it smolder in the ashtray. She felt the alcohol's relaxing warmth, and they raised their glasses to Evan. After another round of drinks, she brought out a picture album and told Lucas the story of their marriage. She felt a familiar melancholy arise, and soon the tears were again flowing.

They fell into silence, each absorbed in their own thoughts. "I'm going to end my husband's life tomorrow," she said.

"You're committing a selfless act of love, one of the highest order," he said softly. "You'd want him to do the same for you."

"Sounds noble," she said. "Doesn't feel that way."

"It's been a long journey," he said, "for both of you."

"I know it's time. His pain will be gone, and he'll go on to something better." She paused and raised the glass to her lips, then looked skyward. "At least I hope so. I can't stop thinking about what he'll experience at the end."

"You mean the afterlife?"

"If there is one," she said. "You teach philosophy, right?"

"I do."

"What do you philosophers say about the subject?"

Lucas gazed into his whiskey a long moment before responding. "People in my line of work have wrestled with this question for eons," he said. "We rarely agree on an answer. The topic of the afterlife is one of two essay questions I always include on my undergraduate midterm examination. I require my students to offer their theories on what happens after we die. Does physical death represent the end of one's existence?"

"Any of your students come up with the right answer?"

"Nobody gets it wrong," he said with a smile.

"What about your personal beliefs?"

"Remember we grew up in the country," he said, "so my views are rooted in fundamental Christianity. I believe there's truth in the Bible and that Jesus walked this earth. I believe with all my heart that Evan's in God's hands. Tomorrow he'll go to a place of peace, and I'll see him again one day."

"So he's going to Heaven?"

"No doubt in my mind," he said.

"By the way, what's the other question?"

He gave her a puzzled look.

"You put two questions on your midterm. What's the other one?"

"Prove the existence of God," he said, "in a hundred words or less. You'd get a kick out of some of their answers." He refilled his glass and raised it to her. "I've bared my soul, and now it's your turn."

"My friend Rose," she said, "also lost her husband in the plane crash. That's how we met, and we've helped each other survive. Rose is a total God fanatic and a little kooky. You'd like her. She adheres to a crazy mix of religions, and her faith is unshakeable. Rose's mission in life is convincing me there is a God. She drags me to church. Preaches to me. We've had our share of heated debates. She's unable to convince me of God's existence, and I can't convince her otherwise."

"You're lucky to have a friend like her," he said. "Where has it all taken you?"

"Still not a total believer," she said. "But I'm more open to the idea of God. I know there are forces greater than us in the world. Too many mysteries. Things that can't be explained by logic or science. Who's to say God's not responsible for it all? And I'm pulling for Rose. I hope she's right, and there's a God and Heaven. I want big pearly gates to swing open when Evan shows up. I want his parents and that old dog he loved so much to come out to greet him. Even if none of that happens, I think his life force goes on in some way. His spirit will fly away to another plane of existence or recycle into nature. Who knows? Maybe we reincarnate. A baby might be born tomorrow at the right moment, and his soul enters its body."

Lucas smiled appreciatively and raised his glass. "That point of view would definitely get a high mark on my midterm." He tilted his head as he thought of something. "There's something else I want to discuss."

He went into the house, and she saw the light go on in the guestroom. He returned carrying the manuscript. He laid it on the table, and his eyes were shiny with emotion as he tapped it with a finger.

"Jeremy's Journey is amazing," he said. "A perfect childhood adventure. I love the characters. The story's filled with metaphor and symbolism."

"I love it, too," she said. "I'm so proud of him for writing it."

"I actually read the manuscript twice. Once for enjoyment, and the second time I examined it from an intellectual standpoint. Let me ask you something. What do you think this story's about?"

"Well, it's an adventure story for kids," she said. "Jeremy gets lost in the woods and tries to find his way home. He meets a girl. They become friends and have adventures. They get into dangerous situations and run from animals that want to harm them. They make friends with bears and rabbits. It's a fun story, filled with magic and mystical creatures."

"I agree with you," he said. "But what's this story really about, on a metaphorical level? Did you pick up an underlying theme?"

She shrugged. "Hadn't thought about it that way. For me, it's a kid's book. Jeremy gets lost and has adventures. You must think there's more to it."

"I didn't intend to put you on the spot," he said. "I'm a philosopher. We're a cursed bunch, and for us nothing ever means what it means. We search for the story that lies beneath the words. I can't just read a book. I have to discover what the author's trying to tell us."

She picked up the manuscript and leafed through it.

"Let's see," she said. "Jeremy's lost. He misses his family and wants to find them. His friend is a runaway and afraid to go home. She wants to stay in the woods." Her eyes widened as she gazed at Lucas.

"This story's about abused children, isn't it?"

"I believe so," he said. "On its surface, this is an adventure story for children. But on another level, Evan was writing about child abuse, how kids experience it, and the ways it affects them. His friend was an abused child, and she ran away because monsters came into her bedroom and hurt her. She wanted to stay in the woods because she felt safe there. Evan did a beautiful job of couching the abuse in metaphor, keeping the reader's focus on fun and adventure. And the ending was perfect. You wrote it?"

"Just the last chapter. I had no idea how he planned to end the story because he never talked with me about it. One weekend last summer, I drank too much wine and decided I'd finish the story for him."

"They find the road that leads them home. But they turn away and return to the woods, where their forest friends are waiting. They go off in search of more adventures."

"Did you like it?"

"It's a perfect ending. One that sets the stage for a series of stories."

"You think somebody would publish it?"

"I have a college chum who works for an agency in New York. If you don't object, I'll send it to him."

They finished their drinks, then hugged and said goodnight. Sarah climbed into bed, head filled with bittersweet memories of the years spent with Evan. The joys and sorrows, the triumphs and tragedies. She remembered the life they had shared, then she thought of him lying alone in his hospital bed.

She turned her thoughts to tomorrow and wondered if she would sleep tonight.

CHAPTER FORTY-ONE

The dirt and gravel two-lane cut a swath through the thick forest, an indelible dividing line separating wilderness from farmers' fields. An overgrown drainage ditch and a string of telephone poles ran in tandem with the road.

He spent an hour standing at its edge. Immobile. Unable to step forward. As if an impenetrable force field stood between him and the way home. He stared at the narrow dirt path and tried to remember the world awaiting him. Sarah. His life and career. He'd spent months trekking through the wilderness, driven by unwavering determination to arrive at this place. Rescue was a three-hour hike away.

He turned to gaze into the woods. Freeze-frame images of Andrea scrolled through his mind. Smiling as she swayed in the firelight. Twirling and dancing among fireflies. Her misty image rising above the waterfall.

She was still out there.

He looked to the west. Towards home.

His thoughts turned to Sarah. He tenderly smiled as he searched his mind for her image. His heart filled with love and appreciation for the life they had shared. Finally, her aura faded and was gone. He knew he would never again see her.

"Goodbye, my love," he said.

He stepped away from the road and into the forest. He'd stay here and resume his search for Andrea. Together they would return to the little cabin.

He stopped to rest in a grassy meadow. Hearing a shuffling sound, he watched as the grizzly emerged from the forest. The animal swiveled its enormous head to gaze at him. He stared into its depthless eyes and at last understood this creature's purpose. It wasn't following him. It wasn't stalking him. It was leading him.

To Andrea? The thought echoed through his mind and resonated in his heart, and he knew it was true. Andrea was still in the woods, following a path she chose to travel alone, seeking her destined place. The grizzly would take him to her.

The grizzly made a chuffing sound as it moved into the forest. He shouldered his backpack and began walking after it.

The hospital room was filled with colorful roses. The delicate Floribunda. The fragrant Iceberg and dramatic French. All gathered from Sarah's carefully tended garden. Friends and neighbors filed through to pay last respects and say their goodbyes. Marcie Malone made a spectacular appearance, decked out in a black miniskirt, matching veil, and spiked heels. Rose Flanagan clutched the big cross on her neck as she hugged Sarah and whispered condolences. Rose went to Evan's bed and took his hand, praying softly into his ear before removing the cross and placing it around his neck. The lawyer Brad Nixon had come and gone, as had Evan's colleagues. Hospital staff stopped in to bid farewell.

Lucas sat beside his brother's body, gently weeping as he said his final goodbyes.

Sarah went in last.

She sat on the edge of the bed, holding the hand of the man she'd sworn to love forever. Whispering her eternal love for him. Thanking him for the life he'd given her. Weeping as she expressed her sorrow for disappointing him. Swearing to keep him in her heart. Wishing him peace on his journey and promising to one day see him again.

Finally, there was nothing more to say.

Grasping the small golden cross on her neck, she whispered a prayer and leaned in close.

"Goodbye, my love," she said.

He rested in the shade of a tall conifer. The grizzly lay nearby, dozing in the morning sun. Evan gazed appreciatively at the bear. He knew where the animal was taking him.

To the shimmering city in the clouds.

He remembered dreaming of the place. Floating on a raft down a lazy river, he'd spotted it towering above his head. People lining the riverbank, arms extended in welcome. He felt an eagerness to arrive in the city. Andrea would run out to greet him. One day, Sarah would join them.

He got to his feet and hefted the backpack. The grizzly rose and they resumed their journey. After a few yards he stopped again, feeling a tightness in his chest. He struggled to fill his lungs, and energy drained from his body. He swayed and fell to the ground, gasping for air.

The bear dropped beside him. He reached out a hand, and the animal extended its big head and allowed him to caress it. The feeling was like nothing he had ever known, as a sense of peace and comfort filled his soul.

He closed his eyes.

At last his journey ended.

FIRST AUTHOR'S NOTE

A compelling story is sometimes born in tragedy.

Late one evening some years ago, I received the dreaded late-night phone call. A friend in crisis, informing me of tragic news. He awoke to find his wife on the floor beside their bed, unconscious and unresponsive. An ambulance rushed her to the hospital in critical and life-threatening condition. We hurried to her bedside, where she appeared to be peacefully sleeping. Doctors later confirmed that an insidious cancer had crept into her brain and devastated it.

Our friend had entered a vegetative state, from which she would never awaken.

We visited her during those final days. Prayed for her. Spoke to her. Encouraged her to awaken and return to us. Although she was unresponsive to us, it seemed her brain was active on some level. Her legs and arms twitched. She clenched her fists. Her lips moved as if she were engaged in conversation. It was evident that she was responding to some internal stimuli. I began to wonder about where her mind had taken her. What she was seeing. What she was experiencing.

Winslow's Journey is a work of fiction, a speculative story based on science and possibility. It is an empirical fact that many comatose patients demonstrate signs of cortical activity. A recent clinical study[1] found that fifteen percent of patients with severe brain injuries exhibited cognitive activation in response to verbal commands, as measured by EEG (electroencephalograph) results. This cortical activity was similar to healthy volunteers responding to the same instructions. Another EEG study[2] demonstrated that the brains of some vegetative patients respond differently to standard and deviant auditory stimulation, suggesting the unconscious mind may possess a greater capacity to track sensory input than previously believed.

Researchers are utilizing functional MRI technology to determine which areas of a comatose patient's brain "light up" when encouraged to imagine specific tasks. This implies a level of awareness and

[1] Jan Claassen, M.D., Kevin Doyle, M.A., Adu Matory, B.A., Caroline Couch, B.A., Kelly M. Burger, B.A., R.E.E.G.T., Angela Velazquez, M.D., Joshua U. Okonkwo, M.D., Jean-Rémi King, Ph.D., Soojin Park, M.D., Sachin Agarwal, M.D., David Roh, M.D., Murad Megjhani, Ph.D., et al., Detection of Brain Activation in Unresponsive Patients with Acute Brain Injury, New England Journal Of Medicine, June 27, 2019.

[2] Athina Tzovara, Alexandre Simonin, Mauro Oddo, Andrea O. Rossetti, Marzia De Lucia, Neural detection of complex sound sequences in the absence of consciousness, *Brain*, Volume 138, Issue 5, May 2015.

raises the possibility of reciprocal communication. One researcher[3] suggested that flat-lined patients showed minimum but wide-spread neural activity, while another study[4] found the presence of spontaneous cortical activity in deeply comatose patients. Researchers worldwide utilize brain imaging technology to explore the "hidden consciousness" of patients in persistent vegetative states. There are countless instances of recorded cortical arousal in the comatose brain. In most of these cases, researchers have no idea what the mind is doing.

Other human experiences confirm cortical activity in the unconscious mind. We experience vivid and complex dreams during sleep. Sleepwalkers engage in brain-directed physical activity such as driving a car or preparing a meal. Near-death survivors tell stories of crossing over into the afterlife, entering lush gardens, reuniting with deceased relatives, or meeting God. Anesthesia awareness is a condition that occurs when surgical patients, during a chemically induced coma, accurately remember details of procedures and conversations among doctors.

The tragic circumstances of my friend's passing inspired me to write Winslow's journey, and I will

---

[3] Bahar Gholipour, From the deepest coma, new brain activity found, Live Science, September 18, 2013.

[4] T. Ganes, T. Lundar, EEG and evoked potentials in comatose patients with severe brain damage, Electroencephalography And Clinical Neurophysiology, Volume 69, Issue 1, January 1988.

forever be grateful. The process not only resulted in a story I enjoyed writing, it led me on a personal journey of reflection, self-exploration, and discovery. Winslow's Journey is a story about the end of life. In writing it, I wrestled with the same philosophical questions as Evan and Sarah Winslow.

I hope there is truth in my fiction, and that my friend's unconscious mind transported her to a place of wonder. I hope she traveled through peaceful forests, floated above misty waterfalls, and danced among the fireflies.

Most of all, I hope her journey took her to a place of eternal peace.

SECOND AUTHOR'S NOTE

Those who have read **Third Messenger** know I was named after two beloved uncles tragically killed within months of each other in World War II. As homage to these heroes, I include their story in every book I write.

During the morning hours of June 6, 1944, Army PFC James Homer Hobbs waded onto the sands of Normandy Beach. He walked into battle alongside his comrades, and minutes later was struck down by heavy shelling. PFC Hobbs was posthumously awarded a Purple Heart and Silver Star. He sacrificed his life in defense of our nation. He was twenty-six, and my mother's youngest brother.

On March 5, 1945, Marine Corporal Ellsworth Patterson Huddleston stepped onto another sandy beach, this one rimming the Pacific island of Okinawa. Within hours, he fell before fierce enemy fire. Corporal Huddleston was posthumously decorated for his bravery. He made the ultimate sacrifice in defense of our nation. He was twenty-seven, and my father's youngest brother.

Each of my parents lost a brother to war, both men dying scant months apart. I struggle to comprehend the depth of my parents' sorrow and grief in the face of such tragedy. My mother has since passed on, and I have no doubt she experienced a joyful reunion with her loved ones. I was born following the war and never had the privilege of knowing these men. My parents chose to honor their memory by bestowing their names upon me. It has taken me a lifetime to fully understand the gift they gave me.

In tribute to these heroes, I write as Ellsworth James.

ACKNOWLEDGMENTS

I am blessed to have Ms. Jane Bornstein as a friend and sounding board. You read an early draft of Winslow's Journey, then you composed and wrote a seven-page letter filled with ideas and suggestions. Imagine someone taking the effort to read a sloppy manuscript, hand-write a lengthy letter and send it by snail-mail! That's friendship. I hope you recognize your contributions to the final version. Thank you, Jane.

My good friend and golfing buddy Shige Baker read a second draft and provided valuable feedback and ideas. When you said the story touched you emotionally, I knew I was on the right track. Thanks, Shige.

Thanks to Parker Sheley, the talented Chicago graphic artist who designed covers for **Third Messenger** and **Winslow's Journey**. I provided you the scarcest of ideas and you converted them into art. Working with you has allowed me to witness creativity in action. Thanks, Parker.

Todd Sudick. Lifelong friend, founding member of the Newlin Street Boys, and one of the world's great aviators. Thanks for your help and insights regarding dead bugs, flight paths and pilot-controller jargon.

Thanks and appreciation to Claudia Tolmie, another forever friend and incredible human being who helped me understand the rituals and symbolism of the Catholic mass, described in Chapter Twenty-Eight.

John and Fiona Nickerson. Great friends and golfing partners. Thanks for your encouragement and support. Thanks for helping me realize my first novel, Third Messenger, was worth reading. For buying copies and handing them out to friends. For connecting me with the book club. For showing up at the writer's symposium. For you, acts of friendship. For me, inspiration to keep writing.

Kathleen. My wife, life partner, and ideal reader, as Stephen King refers to his Tabitha. Your name should stand beside mine as co-author. The version of Winslow's Journey I handed you was ragged and unpolished. The one you edited and returned to me was magic. I struggle to find words that express my feelings or describe the joy and comfort you provide as my wife and life partner. You are my everything. I love you and always will. F.A.T.E.

Finally, thanks to you, the readers of Winslow's Journey. I hope you enjoyed it. If you want to provide any feedback or discuss the story, I'd love to hear from you. Contact me at my website: www.ellsworthjames.com.

Printed in the United States
By Bookmasters